Russian fairy-tales

RUSSIAN FAIRY-TALES
PALEKH PAINTING

RUSSIAN
Fairy – Tales

PALEKH PAINTING

by
Alexei Orleansky

P-2 Art Publishers
St Petersburg

*T*he work of Palekh artists must be counted among the true wonders of Russian art. When you look at their creations on black lacquer backgrounds each of them seems to glisten and sparkle with gold, silver and all the colours of the rainbow, like a feather dropped by the Fire-Bird in the well-known Russian fairy tale. These fabulous hand-made creations have their real-life origins in the depths of Russia.

Palekh is the name of an age-old Russian settlement located on the banks of the River Paleshka, close to Shuya, a town some 190 miles north-east of Moscow.

The settlement dates back to the fourteenth or fifteenth century and it is probable that even then it was an icon-painting centre. In any case, we still have some icons from that period painted in the distinctive manner associated with Palekh. From the first icons were painted on cypress-wood panels or on a papier-mâché base. Gradually icon-painting and its associated crafts became the main industry in Palekh, determining the whole pattern of life and spiritual atmosphere of the place. In the middle of the eighteenth century, the wealth and standing of Palekh found visible expression with the building, in 1762-74, of the masonry Church of the Exultation of the Cross. In 1807 its interior was painted by local artists under the guidance of the Sapozhnikov brothers, masters from Moscow.

In 1894 Palekh had 1,431 inhabitants in 214 households and a school as well as a church; 250 "adult males" were engaged in icon-painting, as well as 120 youths. Up to 10,000 icons were despatched annually to all parts of Russia, their prices ranging from one rouble to one hundred and more.

In 1921—25, when it became clear that icons could no longer be produced or sold, a group of hereditary artists formed the Palekh artel or team of traditional painting which began to specialise in functional papier- mâché items. Their range gradually came to include caskets and boxes, cigarette-cases, trays and brooches, all richly decorated with bright egg-tempera paints on a black lacquer background. Thus the distinctive Palekh miniature emerged as a form of folk art founded on a centuries-old icon-painting tradition. We owe a tremendous debt to the Palekh artists for preserving the techniques of manufacturing their articles and the manner of painting, treatment of figures, landscape and details, and so on. Their works combine traditions and devices derived from icon-painting with subjects inspired by literature,

The Wonder of Palekh

secular and fairy-tale motifs. The functional articles were made only from papier-mâché – pressed paper pulp that has been soaked in glue and other additives. After complex, laborious preparation, the outer surface of the item is covered in black lacquer, the inner surface in red. Then the item is passed to the artist who applies the decoration on top of the lacquer. The design is carefully marked out in white and only then does the work with colours begin. The range of colours is enriched by the use of ground gold leaf. Each section of the painting – down to the finest ornamental details, applied using a magnifying-glass – is subordinated to the overall compositional concept and the single colour-scheme.

Works by Palekh artists can be found in major state collections, such as the Tretyakov Gallery in Moscow and the Russian Museum in St Petersburg, as well as in private collections in Russia and abroad. The subjects are drawn from old epic poems, folk tales and songs. Palekh artists have also turned their hands to book illustration and theatrical set design. Books illustrated by Palekh craftsmen are works of art in their own right and rarities often sought by collectors.

The present publication of Russian folk tales is a remarkable example of this interesting facet of Russian art. The illustrations are by Alexei Orleansky, a painter of the Palekh school. Working with a variety of materials, in 1999 he produced a series of original miniatures illustrating traditional stories. I am sure that his iridescent Fire-Bird colours will bring joy to many readers, young and old.

Abram Raskin,
art scholar,
Merited Art Worker of Russia

Палех   Н.Орабанский 1999 г.

At the Pike's Behest

Once upon a time there was an old man who had three sons. Two of them were bright fellows, the third, called Yemélia, was a bit of a fool. While his brothers worked, Yemelia spent the whole day lying on the stove and took no interest in anything.

One day Yemelia's two brothers had gone to the market, and their wives decided to send him for water.

"Fetch some water, Yemelia."

But he called down from the stove:

"I don't feel like it."

"Fetch some water, or you won't get anything tasty when your brothers come back from the market."

"Oh, all right then."

Yemelia climbed down off the stove, pulled on his coat and boots, took a couple of buckets and an axe and went down to the stream. He broke a hole in the ice, filled the buckets and put them on the bank. He looked into the hole in the ice and spotted a pike in the water. He dropped down and somehow managed to catch hold of the pike and pull it out.

"This will make fine fish soup!"

Suddenly the pike spoke to him in a human voice:

"Yemelia, put me back in the water, I shall be of use to you."

Yemelia just laughed:

"Now how can you be of use to me? No, I'll take you home and my brothers' wives can turn you into soup. You'll make fine soup."

The pike begged him again:

"Yemelia, o Yemelia. Put me back in the water and I shall do everything you ask."

"Very well, but first prove that you are not deceiving me, then I'll let you go."

The pike replied:

"Yemelia, tell me what you want just now."

"I want… I want the buckets to take themselves home, and not spill a drop of water."

The pike said:

"Remember these words, and when you want something just say:

"At my request,
At the pike's behest."

Yemelia repeated after him:

"At my request,
At the pike's behest —

buckets, take yourselves off home."

As soon as he had spoken, the buckets stirred and headed back up the slope. Yemelia dropped the pike back into the water and followed the buckets.

The buckets passed through the village and everyone who was around stopped and stared. Yemelia walked behind grinning. The buckets went into the house and set themselves down on the bench, while Yemelia climbed back onto the stove.

After a time, his sisters-in-law called out:

"Yemelia, why are you lying down? Go and chop some firewood."

"I don't feel like it."

At the Pike's Behest

At that the joints between the logs of the house sprang apart, the roof shook, one wall fell away and the stove lumbered out into the street and off down the road, straight to the palace.

"Chop some firewood, or you won't get anything tasty when your brothers come back from the market."

Yemelia climbed unwillingly down from the stove. Then he remembered about the pike and quietly said:

"At my request,
At the pike's behest —

go, axe, and chop wood, and firewood come into the house and stack yourself by the stove."

The axe sprang up from under the bench, flew out into the yard and chopped the wood in the blinking of an eye. The chopped wood came inside and stacked itself by the stove.

After a time, Yemelia's sisters-in-law called out:

"Yemelia, we've run right out of wood. Go into the forest and cut some."

But he called down from the stove:

"What are you here for?"

"What do you mean? It's none of our business to go into the forest for wood!"

"I don't feel like it."

"Well then, you won't get anything tasty."

There was nothing for it. Yemelia climbed down off the stove, pulled on his coat and boots, took a rope and an axe. He went out into the yard and sat in the sledge.

"Hey, you, women! Open the gate!"

His sisters-in-law shouted:

"Why are you sitting in the sledge, you fool, when you haven't harnessed up the horse?"

"I don't need a horse!"

The women opened the gate, and Yemelia quietly said:

"At my request,
At the pike's behest —

sledge, carry me to the forest."

The sledge stirred and sped out of the gate so fast that a horseman would have been left behind.

To get to the forest, though, Yemelia had to go through the town and he knocked down quite a few people who failed to get out of the way in time. The townsfolk shouted, "Catch him! Stop him!" but Yemelia urged his sledge on even faster. He came to the forest:

"At my request,
At the pike's behest —

axe, cut down firewood, as dry as you can find; firewood tie yourself in bundles and stack yourself in the sledge."

Then Yemelia had the axe cut him a cudgel so big and heavy he could hardly lift it. He got back on the sledge and:

"At my request,
At the pike's behest —

sledge, carry me back home."

The sledge started back. Again Yemelia had to go through the town where he had knocked people down, but this time they were expecting him. The men seized Yemelia and dragged him from the sledge. They beat and cursed him. Yemelia saw he was in real trouble and quietly said:

"At my request,
At the pike's behest —

up, cudgel, and give them a thrashing."

The heavy cudgel sprang up and battered the men until they fled. Ivan drove home and climbed onto the stove.

In time the Tsar himself came to hear about Yemelia's deeds and he sent one of his officers to find him and bring him to the palace:

The officer drove into the village, came into the house where Yemelia lived and asked:

"Are you Yemelia the Fool?"

"What's it to you?" came the voice from the stove.

"Get dressed quickly. I am to take you to the Tsar."

"I don't feel like it."

At that the officer lost his temper and slapped Yemelia on the cheek.

And Yemelia quietly said:

"At my request,
At the pike's behest —

up, cudgel, and give him a thrashing."

The heavy cudgel sprang up and battered the officer, who barely managed to get away.

The Tsar was surprised that his officer had not managed to deal with Yemelia and called his grandest courtier:

"Fetch Yemelia the Fool here to the palace, or I'll have your head from your shoulders."

The grandest courtier bought raisins, prunes and spice-cakes and went off to the village. He went into the house and there he asked the women what Yemelia liked.

"Our Yemelia likes it when people ask him kindly and promise him a fine caftan — then he'll do whatever you ask."

The grandest courtier gave Yemelia the raisins, prunes and spice-cakes and said:

"Yemelia, my boy, why are you lying here on the stove. Let's go and see the Tsar."

"I'm warm enough where I am."

"Yemelia, my boy, there'll be good things to eat and drink at the palace. Come on, let's go."

"I don't feel like it."

"Yemelia, my boy, the Tsar will give you a fine caftan, and a hat and boots."

Yemelia thought and thought.

"Very well. You go on ahead, and I shall be right behind you."

The grandest courtier drove off, but Yemelia stayed lying down and just said:

"At my request,
At the pike's behest —

stove, carry me to the Tsar."

At that the joints between the logs of the house sprang apart, the roof shook, one wall fell away and the stove lumbered out into the street and off down the road, straight to the palace.

The Tsar happened to look out of the window and was astonished:

"What's this wonder?"

The greatest courtier replied:

"That's Yemelia coming to see you on his stove."

The Tsar went out onto the porch:

"Well, Yemelia, I've heard a lot of complaints against you. You knocked down a lot of people."

"Why did they get in front of my sledge?"

At that moment the Tsar's daughter, Princess Maria, looked out of the window. Yemelia saw her in the window and said quietly:

"At my request,
At the pike's behest —

make the Tsar's daughter fall in love with me..."

Then he added:

"And, stove, carry me home."

The stove turned around and went back home. It entered the house and settled back in its place. Yemelia carried on lying there as before.

Meanwhile the Tsar's palace was full of sighs and tears. Princess Maria was longing for Yemelia. She said she could not live without him and begged her father to let her marry him. The Tsar was greatly disturbed and irritated and called his grandest courtier once again:

"Go and fetch Yemelia here, alive or dead, or I'll have your head from your shoulders."

The grandest courtier bought sweet wines and different delicacies and went off to the village. He went into the house and regaled Yemelia with all of them. Yemelia ate and drank his fill, then turned over and fell fast asleep. The grandest courtier carried him out to his carriage and drove him to the palace.

The Tsar immediately ordered his men to bring a large barrel with iron hoops. They placed Yemelia and Princess Maria inside, sealed the barrel up and tossed it into the sea.

Eventually the buffeting woke Yemelia up. He found himself somewhere dark and cramped and groaned:

"Where on earth am I?"

"Alas, dear Yemelia," a voice answered, "we have been sealed up in a barrel and thrown into the sea."

"And who are you?"

"I am Princess Maria."

Then Yemelia said:

"At my request,
At the pike's behest —

strong winds, drive this barrel to the shore, onto the yellow sands."

The strong winds blew. The sea rose and tossed the barrel out onto the shore, onto the yellow sands. Yemelia and the Princess climbed out.

"Dear Yemelia, where shall we live? Build us some kind of a hut."

"I don't feel like it."

The Princess begged him to do it, and he said:

"At my request,
At the pike's behest —

build me a palace of stone with a roof of gold."

No sooner had he spoken, than a palace of stone appeared with a roof of gold. All around it was a green garden with flowers blooming and birds singing.

Princess Maria and Yemelia went inside and sat by one of the windows.

"Dear Yemelia, couldn't you become handsome?"

Yemelia did not stop long to think:

"At my request,
At the pike's behest —

turn me into a fine figure of a man, a sight for sore eyes."

And Yemelia became fairer in face and body than can be imagined or described.

Just then the Tsar was out hunting when he noticed a palace standing where there had been nothing before.

"Who has dared to build a palace on my land without my permission?"

And he sent some of his courtiers to find out.

The messengers rode into the garden and called up to the window.

Yemelia leaned out and said:

"Ask the Tsar to come and be my guest. I shall tell him everything myself."

The Tsar accepted the invitation. Yemelia met him, conducted him into the palace and brought him to the dining-room. They sat down to a feast. The Tsar ate and drank, marvelling all the time:

"But who are you, my fine young sir?"

"You remember Yemelia the Fool who came to see you on a stove and you had him and your daughter sealed up in a barrel and thrown into the sea. I am that selfsame Yemelia. If the fancy takes me, I can burn and ruin your whole kingdom."

The Tsar was terrified at that and began begging forgiveness:

"Marry my daughter, dear Yemelia. Take my kingdom, only spare me!"

There was a great feast to which everyone was invited. Yemelia married Princess Maria and began to rule the kingdom.

Now the tale has all been told; if you were listening you're as good as gold.

The Turnip

Grandpa planted a turnip and said:
"Grow turnip, grow. Grow up strong and sweet."
And it grew as strong and as sweet as can be, the biggest turnip you ever did see.
Grandpa went out to pull up the turnip.
He took tight hold of the turnip top
And he pulled and pulled till he had to stop.
But the turnip stayed in the ground.

Then Grandpa called Grandma.
Grandma held onto Grandpa;
Grandpa held tight to the turnip top.
They pulled and pulled till they had to stop.
But the turnip stayed in the ground.

Then Grandma called their granddaughter Ánya.
Anya held onto Grandma;
Grandma held onto Grandpa;
Grandpa held tight to the turnip top.
They pulled and pulled till they had to stop.
But the turnip stayed in the ground.

Then Anya called their dog named Dánya.
Danya held onto Anya;
Anya held onto Grandma;
Grandma held onto Grandpa;
Grandpa held tight to the turnip top.
They pulled and pulled till they had to stop.
But the turnip stayed in the ground.

Then Danya called their cat named Sánya.
Sanya held onto Danya;
Danya held onto Anya;
Anya held onto Grandma;
Grandma held onto Grandpa;
Grandpa held tight to the turnip top.
They pulled and pulled till they had to stop.
But the turnip stayed in the ground.

Then Sanya called a little mouse.
The mouse held onto Sanya;
Sanya held onto Danya;
Danya held onto Anya;
Anya held onto Grandma;
Grandma held onto Grandpa;
Grandpa held tight to the turnip top.
They pulled and pulled and suddenly — pop!
The turnip came out of the ground!

Палех   А. Орлеанский 1999 г.

The Peasant and the Bear

A peasant man went into the forest to plant turnips. He cleared a plot and dug it over. Just then a bear came up to him and said:

"Man, I am going to thrash you."

"Don't thrash me, dear bear. You'd do better to let me plant my turnips. When they grow, we'll share. You take the tops, but let me at least keep the roots."

"Very well," said the bear. "But if you deceive me, you had better not show your face in the forest again".

With that he turned and went back into the thick forest.

The turnips grew large and in the autumn the peasant came with his cart to dig them up. The bear came out of the thick forest:

"Well, man, the time has come to divide the turnips. Give me my share."

"All right, dear bear, let's share: the tops for you, the roots for me."

The peasant gave the bear all the leafy tops, put the turnips on his cart and took them off to town to sell.

On the way he came across the bear again:

"Where are you going, man?"

"I am going to town, dear bear, to sell the roots."

"Well, let my try one to see what it is like."

The peasant gave him a turnip. The bear took a big bite and roared:

"Rrrrr! You have tricked me! Your roots are nice and sweet! Don't come into the forest for firewood or I shall thrash you!"

The next year the peasant planted rye on the same spot.

When he came to reap it, he found the bear already waiting for him:

"You won't trick me this time, man. Give me my share."

The peasant said:

"Very well. You take the roots, dear bear, but let me at least keep the tops."

They gathered the rye. The peasant left the bear the roots, loaded the rye onto his cart and took it home.

The bear tried everything, but he could not find any use for the roots. He was furious with the peasant and since then there has always been hostility between bear and man.

The Cockerel with the Golden Crest

Once upon a time there were a cat, a thrush and a cockerel with a golden crest who all lived together in a little wooden house in the forest.

One day the cat and the thrush went out to cut firewood, leaving the cockerel on his own. As they left, they warned him:

"We are going far off and you will be here alone looking after the house. When the cunning fox comes past, be sure the window stays shut fast."

The fox soon found out that the cat and the thrush were not at home. He ran to the wooden house, sat down under the window and sang out:

"O cockerel with your golden crest,
Your glorious hackles and silky breast,
Open the window, won't you please,
And I shall give you your fill of peas."

When he heard that, the cockerel put his head out of the window. Quick as a flash the fox grabbed him and hurried away home.

The frightened cockerel called out:

"The fox is carrying me to his lair
Through forests dark and mountains bare
Over rivers that flow fast and free…
Come cat, come thrush, and rescue me!"

The cat and the thrush heard him, dashed after the fox and managed to get the cockerel away from him.

When the time came for the cat and the thrush to go into the forest again for firewood, they told the cockerel:

"This time be sure not to look out of the window, as we are going even farther away and will not hear you if you call."

They went away and soon the fox again appeared beneath the window and sang:

"O cockerel with your golden crest,
Your glorious hackles and silky breast,
Open the window, won't you please,
And I shall give you your fill of peas."

The cockerel kept quiet and still, so the fox went on:

"The children came merrily,
Scattering the corn about.
The hens they eat it happily,
But cockerels must go without."

At that the cockerel stuck his head out of the window and cackled:
"What, what, what? What do you mean 'go without'?"
The fox grabbed him and hurried away home.
The frightened cockerel called out:

Палех   А Орлеанский 1999.

"The fox is carrying me to his lair
Through forests dark and mountains bare
Over rivers that flow fast and free…
Come cat, come thrush, and rescue me!"

The cat and the thrush heard him and dashed after the fox. The cat ran as fast as he could; the thrush flew swiftly above the wood. They caught up with the fox. The thrush fluttered and pecked, the cat scratched and bit to good effect — and they got the cockerel away.

After some time the cat and the thrush had to go into the forest for firewood again. As they left they warned the cockerel as strongly as they could:

"Don't listen to the fox. Don't look out of the window. We are going even farther and will not hear if you call."

Off they went into the forest. As soon as they had gone, the fox was back. He sat beneath the window and sang:

"O cockerel with your golden crest,
Your glorious hackles and silky breast,
Open the window, won't you please,
And I shall give you your fill of peas."

The cockerel kept quiet and still, so the fox went on:

"The children came merrily,
Scattering the corn about.
The hens they eat it happily,
But cockerels must go without."

Still the cockerel kept quiet, so the fox went on:

"People came merrily
Scattering nuts about
The hens they eat them happily,
But cockerels must go without."

At that the cockerel stuck his head out of the window and cackled:

"What, what, what? What do you mean 'go without'?"

The fox grabbed him tight and hurried through forests dark and mountains bare, over rivers that flow fast and free, all the way to his lair.

The frightened cockerel called and called, but all in vain. The cat and the thrush did not hear him and it was only when they returned home that they found he was gone.

The pair hurried after the fox. The cat ran as fast as he could, the thrush flew swiftly above the wood… and they came to the fox's lair. The cat took his *gúsli* — a stringed instrument a bit like a zither — and began to play:

"Hum, *gusli*, sing,
String upon golden string.

Here is the fox's cosy lair.
I wonder, will we find him there."

The fox listened and thought to himself:
"I'll just take a look who is playing the *gusli* so well and singing so sweetly."
He climbed out of his lair and the cat and the thrush pounced on him. They fluttered and bit, scratched and pecked until he gave up and ran away.
They found the cockerel, sat him in a basket and carried him back home.
The three of them never had any more trouble from the fox and they are still living happily together today.

Ivan-Tsarevich and the Grey Wolf

Once upon a time there was a Tsar named Berendéi who had three sons, the youngest of which was named Ivan. Now this Tsar had a splendid garden and the most splendid thing about it was an apple-tree with golden apples.

Somebody began to visit the Tsar's garden and steal the golden apples. The Tsar was upset and sent guards to keep watch over the garden. Yet however many he sent, they could not catch the thief.

The Tsar became quite tormented by this business and even stopped eating and drinking. His sons tried to comfort him:

"Dear father, do not be sad, we shall go and keep watch ourselves."

The eldest son said:

"Tonight it is my turn. I shall go and guard the garden from the thief."

And off he went. For all he prowled about that evening, he did not see anyone. Eventually he lay down on the soft grass and fell asleep.

In the morning the Tsar asked him:

"Well, do you have any good news for me? Did you see the thief?"

"No, father dear, I stayed awake the whole night, didn't close an eye, but I never saw anyone."

The next night the middle son went to keep watch. He too slept the whole night through and in the morning said he had not seen the thief.

The time came for the youngest son to go and keep watch. Ivan went to guard his father's garden and was afraid even to sit, let alone lie down. When he felt his eyelids becoming heavy, he washed them with dew from the grass and was wide awake again.

He had watched half the night when suddenly it seemed to him that there was a light in the garden. It grew brighter and brighter until the whole garden was lit up. There on the apple-tree he saw the Fire-Bird pecking at the golden fruit.

Ivan-Tsarevich crept quietly up to the tree and grabbed the bird by its tail. The Fire-Bird took fright and flew away, and Ivan was left with a single feather from its tail in his hand.

In the morning Ivan-Tsarevich came to his father.

"Well, my dear son, did you see the thief?"

"Father dear, I did not catch him, but, yes, I saw who is ruining our garden. Here I have brought you a souvenir of the thief. It is the Fire-Bird!"

The Tsar took the feather and from that moment he began eating and drinking again and forgot about his sorrow. After a while he started thinking about the Fire-Bird. He called his sons to him and said:

"My dear children, why don't you saddle up some good horses and ride out into the world, take a look what it is like and see if you can find this Fire-Bird."

The three brothers took their leave, saddled up three good horses and set out, the eldest in one direction, the next in another, and Ivan-Tsarevich in a third.

Ivan-Tsarevich rode for quite a time. It was a fine summer's day and he began to feel tired. He climbed off his horse, tied it up and dropped off to sleep.

After a while, Ivan woke up and realised that his horse had gone. He set off to look for it, walked and walked, and finally found a heap of bare bones — all that remained of his horse.

Ivan-Tsarevich was dismayed. He had so far to go and now he was without a horse.

"Well, so what," he though to himself. "I said I would, so I shall have to."

And he set off on foot.

He walked and walked until he was dead tired. Then he sat down on the soft grass and hung his head.

From out of nowhere a grey wolf came running up to him:

"Why do you sit and hang your head, Ivan-Tsarevich?"

Ivan-Tsarevich and the Grey Wolf

The Grey Wolf tore along with Ivan-Tsarevich and Yelena the Beautiful on his back. He moved at such a pace that the forests were just a blur and the lakes and rivers swept past beneath his tail.

"I've every reason to be sad, Grey Wolf. I have lost my good horse."

"It was I, Ivan-Tsarevich, who ate your horse… I am sorry for you. Tell me why you were travelling so far and where you are bound."

"My father sent me out to travel the world and to find the Fire-Bird."

"Huh! You and your good horse would never have reached the Fire-Bird in three years. I alone know where it lives. Very well — I have eaten your horse, so I shall serve you loyally and truly. Get on my back and hold tight."

Ivan-Tsarevich got onto the wolf's back and the Grey Wolf took off at such a pace that the forests were just a blur and the lakes swept past beneath his tail. After quite some time they reached a tall fortress. The Grey Wolf stopped and said:

"Listen carefully, Ivan-Tsarevich, and mark my words. You have to climb over the wall — don't worry; this is a good moment as all the guards are asleep. In a tower you will see a window; in the window stands a golden cage and in the cage the Fire-Bird sits. Take the bird, put it into the breast of your clothing, but be sure not to touch the cage!"

Ivan-Tsarevich climbed the wall and saw the tower. The golden cage did indeed stand in the window and there inside was the Fire-Bird. He took the bird, tucked it into the breast of his clothing and then looked at the cage. He looked and marvelled. "How beautiful and how costly it is! What a shame not to take it," he thought — and forgot what the wolf had said. The moment his hand touched the cage, the fortress was filled with noise: trumpets sounded, drums rolled, the guards awoke. They seized Ivan-Tsarevich and brought him before Tsar Afron.

Tsar Afron was enraged and demanded to know who he was and where he came from.

"I am Tsar Berendei's son, Ivan-Tsarevich."

"What a disgrace! A Tsar's son and he goes out thieving!"

"And what about your bird that came and plundered our garden?"

"If you had come to me and asked properly, I would have given the bird to you, out of respect for your parent, Tsar Berendei — but now I shall have it cried everywhere what a rogue you are… All right then, if you perform one task for me, I shall forgive you. In such-and-such a kingdom Tsar Kusman has a horse with a golden mane. Bring me that horse and I shall give you the Fire-Bird and the cage as well".

Ivan-Tsarevich went back downcast to find the Grey Wolf. And the wolf said:

"I told you not to touch the cage! Why didn't you listen to my instructions?"

"I'm sorry. Forgive me, Grey Wolf."

"Sorry, is it…Oh well, get on my back again. Never let it be said that I leave things half done."

Again the Grey Wolf ran off with Ivan-Tsarevich. After quite some time they reached the fortress where the horse with the golden mane was to be found.

"Climb over the wall, Ivan-Tsarevich, while the guards are sleeping. Go to the stables, take the horse, but on no account touch the bridle!"

Ivan climbed into the fortress. All the guards were asleep. He made his way into the stables, found the horse with the golden mane, and then he caught sight of the bridle — it was made of gold and decorated with precious stones, indeed the only thing that could be put on such a horse.

Ivan-Tsarevich reached for the bridle and the fortress was filled with noise: trumpets sounded, drums rolled, the guards awoke. They seized Ivan-Tsarevich and brought him before Tsar Kusman.

"Who are you and where are you from?"

"I am Ivan-Tsarevich."

"Well, well, and look what you have been up to! Horse-stealing — even a common peasant would know better than that. All right then, if you perform one task for me, I shall forgive you. Tsar Dalmat has a daughter called Yeléna the Beautiful. Carry her off and bring her to me and I shall give you the horse

with the golden mane and the bridle as well".

Ivan-Tsarevich went back even more downcast to find the Grey Wolf.

"I told you not to touch the bridle. Why didn't you listen to my instructions?"

"I'm sorry. Forgive me, Grey Wolf,"

"Sorry, is it... Oh well, get on my back again."

Again the Grey Wolf ran off with Ivan-Tsarevich. They ran as far as Tsar Dalmat's fortress and there in the garden Yelena the Beautiful used to walk with her nurses and nannies. The Grey Wolf said:

"This time I shall leave you here and go myself. You start back the way we came and I shall soon catch up with you."

Ivan-Tsarevich set off back the way they had come, while the Grey Wolf leapt over the wall and into the garden. He crouched behind a bush and waited... Yelena the Beautiful came out with her nurses and nannies. They strolled and strolled, and the moment Yelena the Beautiful fell a little behind her nurses and nannies, the Grey Wolf pounced, tossed her over his back and was gone.

Ivan-Tsarevich was walking along when suddenly the Grey Wolf caught up with him and there on the wolf's back was Yelena the Beautiful. Ivan-Tsarevich was overjoyed, but the Grey Wolf said:

"Get on my back quickly, in case they come after us!"

The Grey Wolf tore along with Ivan-Tsarevich and Yelena the Beautiful on his back. He moved at such a pace that the forests were just a blur and the lakes and rivers swept past beneath his tail. After a time they came near Tsar Kusman's fortress. The Grey Wolf asked:

"Why so quiet Ivan-Tsarevich? Is there something on your mind?"

"Of course I am unhappy, Grey Wolf. How can I bear to part with such a maiden? How can I exchange Yelena the Beautiful for a horse?"

The Grey Wolf replied:

"I won't part you from such beauty. We shall hide her somewhere here. I shall turn myself into Yelena the Beautiful and you bring me to the Tsar."

So they hid Yelena the Beautiful in a hut in the forest. The Grey Wolf turned head-over-heels and became the spit and image of Yelena the Beautiful. Ivan-Tsarevich brought her to Tsar Kusman. The Tsar was delighted and thanked him profusely:

"Thank you, Ivan-Tsarevich, for bringing me my bride. Take the horse with the golden mane and the bridle as well."

Ivan-Tsarevich mounted the horse and rode back to Yelena the Beautiful. He sat her in front of him on the horse and rode on.

Tsar Kusman meanwhile arranged his wedding. The feasting went on into the evening and when it came time he carried his bride up to the bedchamber. He lay her down on the bed and as he looked into her face he saw — a wolf's snout and fangs! The Tsar fell back in fear and the wolf made good his escape.

The Grey Wolf caught up with Ivan-Tsarevich and asked him:

"Is there something on your mind?"

"Of course, Grey Wolf. How can I bear to part with such a treasure? How can I exchange the horse with a golden mane for the Fire-Bird?"

"Don't despair, I shall help you."

So, as they came near Tsar Afron's fortress, the wolf said:

"You hide this horse and Yelena the Beautiful. I shall turn myself into the horse with the golden mane and you bring me to the Tsar."

They hid Yelena the Beautiful and the horse with the golden mane in the forest. The Grey Wolf turned head-over-heels and became the spit and image of the horse with the golden mane. Ivan-Tsarevich brought it to Tsar Afron. The Tsar was delighted and gave him the Fire-Bird together with its golden cage.

Ivan-Tsarevich returned on foot to the forest, sat Yelena the Beautiful on the horse with the golden mane, took up the Fire-Bird in its golden cage and rode off towards his own country.

Meanwhile Tsar Afron gave orders for the horse to be brought out and was about to mount it, when it turned back into the Grey Wolf. The Tsar fell back in fear and the Grey Wolf made good his escape.

Soon he caught up with Ivan-Tsarevich and said:

"Now I bid you farewell, as I can go no further."

Ivan-Tsarevich sprang from his horse and bowed deeply three times, thanking the Grey Wolf with great respect. But the wolf said:

"Do not take your last leave of me, you will have need of me again."

Ivan-Tsarevich thought "What more need can I have of him? All my wishes have come true."
He mounted the horse with the golden mane and rode on with Yelena the Beautiful and the Fire-Bird.
He had reached familiar places, when he decided to stop for lunch. He had a little food with him and they washed it down with cool spring water. Then they lay down to rest.

As soon as Ivan-Tsarevich had fallen asleep, his brothers came riding up. They had travelled through other lands, seeking the Fire-Bird and were now returning empty-handed. When they saw all that Ivan-Tsarevich was bringing back, they plotted together:

"Let us kill our brother and all this will be ours."

And they did kill Ivan-Tsarevich, mounted the horse with the golden mane and took the Fire-Bird. They sat Yelena the Beautiful on one of their own horses and threatened her with terrible things if she spoke a word of what they had done.

Ivan-Tsarevich lay dead and the crows were already gathering, when out of nowhere the Grey Wolf appeared and seized a great crow and one of its young.

"You, crow, fly and fetch living and dead water. If you bring me both living and dead water, I shall let your youngster go."

The crow had no choice but to go, as the wolf kept tight hold of the fledgling. After a time the bird came back with living and dead water. The Grey Wolf sprinkled dead water on Ivan-Tsarevich's wounds and they healed. He then sprinkled the prince with living water and Ivan-Tsarevich came back to life.

"Oh, how deeply I slept!"

"Deep indeed," said the wolf. "If it had not been for me, you would never have woken. Your own brothers killed you and carried off all you had gained. Get on my back quickly!"

They went chasing after Ivan's brothers and when they caught up with them the Grey Wolf tore them both apart and scattered the pieces in all directions.

Ivan-Tsarevich bowed again to the Grey Wolf and took his leave of him for ever.

Ivan-Tsarevich returned home on the horse with the golden mane, bringing the Fire-Bird for his father and Yelena the Beautiful for himself.

Tsar Berendei was delighted and began to ask his son about his adventures. Ivan-Tsarevich told him how the Grey Wolf had helped him, how his brothers had killed him as he slept, and how the Grey Wolf had torn them to pieces.

The Tsar was saddened, but soon comforted. Ivan-Tsarevich married Yelena the Beautiful and they lived happily ever after.

Палех   1999г. А.Орлеанский

Masha and the Bear

Once upon a time there was an old man and woman who lived in a village together with their little granddaughter Masha.

One day the village girls decided to go into the forest to gather berries and mushrooms. They came and asked Masha to join them.

"Grandfather, grandmother," Masha said, "may I go into the forest with the village girls?"

And the old couple replied:

"Yes, you may, only be sure to stay with the others so that you don't get lost."

The girls went into the forest and began gathering berries and mushrooms. Little Masha went from tree to tree and from bush to bush, and before long she had wandered far away from the others.

She looked for them and called out their names, but they could not hear her and did not reply.

Little Masha kept walking through the forest, first this way, then that, and became thoroughly lost.

She came right to the heart of the forest, to the densest part, and there stood a little wooden house. Masha knocked on the door, but there was no reply. She pushed on the door, and it opened.

Little Masha went into the wooden house. She sat down on a bench by the window.

As she sat, she thought: "Who can live here? Why is there no-one home?"

The house belonged to a great big bear. He was not at home just then, because he was out walking in the forest.

In the evening the bear came back. He saw little Masha and was delighted.

"Oho," he said, "now I shall keep you here! You will live in my house, feed the stove, make porridge and serve it to me."

Now Masha was very unhappy at this idea, she cried for a time, but she had no choice.

And so she began to live in the bear's wooden house.

The bear would go out into the forest for the whole day, telling Masha not to leave the house while he was away.

"Even if you do go off," he said, "I shall soon find you — and then I shall eat you!"

Little Masha began to think how she could get away from the bear. There was dense forest all around. She did not know which way to go, and there was no-one to ask.

She thought and thought, and came up with an idea.

Once, when the bear came back from walking in the forest, Masha said to him:

"Bear, let me go back to the village for a day. I shall bake some pies and take them to grandmother and grandfather."

"No, no," said the bear, "you will lose your way in the forest. Give me the pies and I shall take them myself."

And that was just what Masha wanted!

She baked the pies, put them in a dish, took down a huge pannier — a basket you wear on your back — and said to the bear:

"Look, I shall put the pies in this basket for you to take to grandmother and grandfather. Only promise not to open the basket on the way and take out the pies. I shall climb to the top of that oak and watch you."

"Very well," the bear replied, "give me the basket."

Then Masha said:

"Just go out on the porch and take a look whether it is raining, would you."

As soon as the bear was outside, Masha leapt into the pannier and pulled the dish of pies in on top of her.

The bear came in and saw that the basket was ready. He swung it onto his back and set off for the village.

The bear wandered past firs. He wandered past birches. Uphill and downhill he went, until he felt tired and said out loud:

"I'll just take the weight off my feet
And have a little pie to eat!"

But Masha called out from the basket:

"I can see you! I can see you!
Don't take the weight off your feet!
Don't have a little pie to eat!
Take them to grandmother!
Take them to grandfather!"

"What eyesight she must have," the bear said. "She can see everything."

He lifted the pannier and kept walking. He walked and walked until he felt really tired. Then he stopped, sat down and said:

"I'll just take the weight off my feet
And have a little pie to eat!"

But Masha called out again from the basket:

"I can see you! I can see you!
Don't take the weight off your feet!
Don't have a little pie to eat!
Take them to grandmother!
Take them to grandfather!"

The bear was astonished:

"You can't outsmart her! She must have climbed way up high to see this far!"

He reached the village, found the house where Masha's grandfather and grandmother lived and knocked on the gate as hard as he could.

Knock, knock. "Open up, open up! I've brought you pies from little Masha."

But the village dogs caught the smell of the bear and came barking and running from every yard. The bear took fright, left the pannier by the gate and hurried back to the forest without looking round.

At that moment Masha's grandmother and grandfather came out to the gate. They looked and saw the big basket.

"What can be in this basket?" the old woman asked.

The old man lifted the lid and simply stared. He could not believe his eyes — there in the pannier sat Masha, whom they had given up for lost, alive and well.

Grandmother and grandfather were delighted. They hugged and kissed Masha and praised her for outwitting the bear.

Kolobok

Once upon a time an old man and woman lived in a village.

One day the old man said to the old woman:

"Grandmother, go scrape in the flour-tin and sweep in the corn bin, perhaps you will get enough flour to make a *kolobók*.»

The old woman went off and scraped round the flour-tin and swept the bottom of the corn-bin and she got a couple of handfuls of flour.

She mixed the flour with sour cream and shaped it into a *kolobok* — a kind of little round bun or cake. Then she fried it in butter and left it on the window-sill to cool.

The *kolobok* lay there for a good while then suddenly it got up and rolled. It rolled from the sill to the bench, from the bench to the floor, across the floor to the door. It hopped over the threshold and into the hall. From the hall it rolled onto the porch, from the porch into the garden and from the garden out through the gate. Further and further it went.

The *kolobok* rolled down the road until it met a hare.

"Ah, *kolobok, kolobok*, I'll eat you now."

"Don't eat me, hare. I'll sing you a song:

I'm *kolobok, kolobok*!
I was scraped up in the flour-tin,
Swept up from the corn-bin,
Mixed with sour cream into a bun
Fried in butter till I was done,
Then left on the sill till I cooled some.
I ran away from grandfather,
I ran away from grandmother too,
And I'm sure I'll have no trouble, hare, running away from you."

And off it rolled down the road, so fast that the hare could only stare.

The *kolobok* rolled down the road until it met a wolf:

"Ah, *kolobok, kolobok*, I'll eat you now."

"Don't eat me, grey wolf. I'll sing you a song:

I'm *kolobok, kolobok*!
I was scraped up in the flour-tin,
Swept up from the corn-bin,
Mixed with sour cream into a bun
Fried in butter till I was done,
Then left on the sill till I cooled some.
I ran away from grandfather,
I ran away from grandmother,
I ran away from the hare too
And I'm sure I'll have no trouble, wolf, running away from you."

And off it rolled down the road, so fast that the wolf could only stare.

The *kolobok* rolled down the road until it met a bear:

"Ah, *kolobok, kolobok*, I'll eat you now."

"Don't eat me, bear. I'll sing you a song:

I'm *kolobok, kolobok*!
I was scraped up in the flour-tin,
Swept up from the corn-bin,
Mixed with sour cream into a bun
Fried in butter till I was done,
Then left on the sill till I cooled some.
I ran away from grandfather,
I ran away from grandmother,
I ran away from the hare
I ran away from the grey wolf too
And I'm sure I'll have no trouble, bear, running away from you."

Again it rolled off down the road, so fast that the bear could only stare.
The *kolobok* rolled down the road until it met a fox:
"*Kolobok, kolobok*, where are you going."
"I'm just rolling along the road."
"*Kolobok, kolobok*, sing me your song."
And the *kolobok* began:

"I'm *kolobok, kolobok*!
I was scraped up in the flour-tin,
Swept up from the corn-bin,
Mixed with sour cream into a bun
Fried in butter till I was done,
Then left on the sill till I cooled some.
I ran away from grandfather,
I ran away from grandmother,
I ran away from the hare
I ran away from the grey wolf
I ran away from the big bear too
And I'm sure I'll have no trouble, fox, running away from you."

But the fox said:
"What a fine song, but, you know, I am rather hard of hearing. *Kolobok*, be so kind as to sit on my nose and sing your song again, a little louder."
The *kolobok* hopped onto the fox's nose and sang the song again a little louder.
But the fox said:
"*Kolobok*, be so kind as to sit on my tongue and sing your song just one more time."
The *kolobok* hopped onto the fox's tongue and — snap! — the fox gobbled it up.

The Flying Ship

Once upon a time there was a couple who had three sons — two sensible lads and a third, Ivan, who was reckoned a fool. The mother loved her sensible sons, dressed them cleanly and fed them with good things, while Vániushka, as he was known, went around in a black shirt and had stale crusts to eat.

One day the Tsar sent out a proclamation to the whole country:

"Whosoever shall build a ship that sails through the skies shall have the hand of the Princess Katerina in marriage."

The two elder brothers decided to go and try their luck. Their mother provided them with clean clothes for the journey. She gave them some fine pies, roast meat and poultry, and white wine and saw them as far as the end of the village.

The brothers walked down the road and came across a crippled old man.

The old man came up to them and said:

"Give a crust of bread to a poor cripple."

But they replied:

"Whatever next! Feed beggars with our mother's fine pies! Treat beggars to roast meat and poultry! There's barely enough for us!"

The old man bowed to them, saying:

"Well, if you have nothing yourselves, there's no question of sharing."

And he went away.

The brothers walked on for an hour or two before they felt hungry. They untied their sacks, looked inside and there, instead of fine pies and roast meat, they found pine-cones and pieces of rotten bark; instead of white wine, they found swamp water. What could they do? You can't go far on an empty stomach.

They debated and argued and in the end went back home to lie on the stove.

Then Vaniushka the Fool decided to set off and try his luck.

His mother gave him some blackened crusts of bread and a bottle of water and saw him as far as the door.

Vaniushka walked and walked and came across the crippled old man.

"Give a crust of bread to a poor cripple, young man."

"I would give you all I have, but I am ashamed to offer burnt crusts."

"That's all right, my son, with a kind word to season it even a blackened crust tastes sweet."

So they sat down and Vaniushka untied his sack.

He looked inside and — oh wonders! — instead of burnt crusts he found fine pies, roast meat and poultry and, in his flask he found white wine.

And so they ate and drank.

The old cripple then asked:

"And where are you headed, Vaniushka?"

"The Tsar has promised to give his daughter to the man who makes a flying ship."

"And can you make a flying ship?"

"No, I can't."

"Then why are you going?"

"There are some good people in this world, perhaps one of them will show me."

"Well, if that's the case, I shall show you. Go into the forest, go up to the first tree, strike it with an axe then throw yourself face down on the ground and wait. If you see a ship fully made, get into it and fly to the palace. Oh, and pick up everyone you meet on the way."

Vaniushka thanked the old man, bade him farewell and went into the forest. He went up to the first tree, struck it a blow with his axe, threw himself down on the ground and fell asleep.

Towards evening Vaniushka woke up and saw a ship fully made resting on the earth. Without pausing to think, Vaniushka leapt into the ship. The ship took off and flew through the air so fast that the tops of the pines and firs were bent where it passed.

Vaniushka flew on and on, then looking down he spotted a man lying in the road with his ear pressed to the ground.

"Greetings, my good fellow."

"Greetings, Vaniushka."

"What are you doing?"

"I am listening to the birds singing beyond the sea."

"Join me on my ship."

"Why not."

And the two of them flew off together.

They flew on and on, then looking down they spotted a man walking on one leg, while his other was tied to his ear.

"Greetings, my good fellow. Why are you hopping along on one leg?"

"If I were to untie the other, then I would cover the whole world with a single step."

"Join us on the ship."

He got aboard and again they flew off.

They flew on and on, then looking down they spotted a man standing with a gun and aiming at something they could not see.

"Greetings, my good fellow. Where are you aiming? There's not a bird in sight."

"I don't shoot at things close by. Give me a beast or a bird a thousand *versts** or so away — that's what I call shooting!"

"Join our company."

He too got aboard and they flew off.

They flew on and on, then looking down they spotted a man carrying a whole sack of bread on his back.

"Greetings, my good fellow. Where are you going?"

"I am going to find bread for my dinner."

"But you already have a whole sack of it!"

"That is hardly a mouthful for me!"

"You will be Never-Fed. Come and join us!"

Never-Fed got aboard and they flew off. They flew on and on, then looking down they spotted a man standing in tears by a lake.

"Hey, my good fellow, what have you lost, why are you crying?"

"I am thirsty and I cannot find water."

"But there's a whole lake in front of you. Why don't you drink?"

"Bah! That will hardly make a mouthful for me!"

"You will be Ever-Parched. Come and join us!"

They were about to fly off when they spotted a man walking along carrying a sheaf of straw.

"Greetings, my good fellow. Where are you taking that straw?"

"To the village."

"Is there no straw then in the village?"

"This is a special sort of straw. Scatter it anywhere hot and it becomes cold enough for snow and ice."

"So that's the way of it! Come aboard, Frost-Strewer, and join us."

By now darkness was coming on and they had begun to settle down for the night when suddenly they spotted another man out and about. He was going into the forest with a bundle of firewood on his back.

---

* Verst — an old Russian measure of distance, just over a kilometre or almost two-thirds of a mile.

"Greetings, my good fellow. Why are you carrying firewood into the forest?"

"This is no ordinary firewood."

"What is it then?"

"Well, if you scatter it, a whole army springs up immediately."

"That's marvellous. Come and join our company."

"Why not. It's more fun than being alone."

So they sat down and were having supper, when suddenly there was a tremendous noise. They looked and there was a man of no great size walking along and tossing a mountain from hand to hand.

"Greetings, Strongman. Come and join us for supper and a bed."

"Why not. I was getting bored on my own."

They slept through the night and in the morning they boarded the ship and flew straight to the royal palace. When they arrived, the Tsar was dining. He saw the flying ship through the window and was astonished. He sent his servant to find out who it was had arrived on the ship.

The servant went up to the ship, and seeing that there was no-one of noble blood aboard, turned round without speaking. He went back and reported to the Tsar that the ship carried neither tsareviches nor princes, but only common people, simple peasants.

The Tsar was greatly disappointed and began to wonder how he could avoid getting a peasant as a son-in-law. He thought hard and long, then he said to himself: "I shall set him a number of impossible tasks."

Keen-Ears, however, had had his head to the ground. He heard what the Tsar said and told Vaniushka:

"You should accept the tasks that the Tsar sets you, we shall perform them for you."

"Very well."

The Tsar came out and said to Ivan:

"Now, my would-be son-in-law, you should show your mettle. Eat, at one sitting, a dozen roast oxen and a dozen stovefuls of bread."

Ivan took fright and said to his companions:

"I can't even finish a single loaf!"

But Never-Fed quickly said:

"Don't worry, Vaniushka. I'll eat it all and still be hungry."

And so the Tsar's servants brought into the room where they were a dozen roast oxen and a dozen stovefuls of white bread.

Never-Fed sat down to this snack. All you could hear was the crunching of bones; all you could see was the loaves flying like birds into his mouth. He ate everything and licked the plate clean.

The Tsar's servants came back and Vaniushka told them:

"You're not very generous with your portions. I can't say I'm hungry, but I'm not really full."

The Tsar was astonished, but he thought up the next task — to drink forty barrels of wine, each which contained forty gallons.

The Tsar's servants rolled in the oaken barrels. Ever-Parched knocked the tops out of the barrels and drank down the wine in a single gulp.

The Tsar's chief servant came back and asked if Vaniushka had finished. Vaniushka replied:

"You're not very generous with your portions. I'm not really drunk, and I'm not really full."

By now the Tsar was getting worried and said to his loyal servant:

"We have to be rid of this peasant. Take him to the bathhouse to wash and have our iron bathhouse heated until it's red-hot… no white-hot! He'll be dead the instant he steps inside."

But Keen-Ears heard everything that passed between them.

The servants invited Vaniushka to the bathhouse, and he said:

The Flying Ship

*T*hen all the companions boarded the flying ship and they sailed
across the great sea to the wonderful island of Buyan.

"My own servant will come with me to scatter straw on the bench."

Frost-Strewer entered the bathhouse with Vaniushka and spread straw on the floor. The bathhouse immediately became as cold as winter. Vaniushka could hardly wash himself, and then he climbed onto the stove and spent the whole night there.

In the morning the Tsar's servants opened the door, thinking to find nothing but a handful of ashes, and there was Vaniushka perched on the stove singing to himself.

The Tsar was really worried and thought up another task — Vaniushka could marry the princess if he brought water from a certain distant well for the Tsar's dinner. If he was late, though, he would lose his head.

Fleet-of-Foot changed clothes with Vaniushka and ran faster than an arrow to that distant well. He took some water in a jug and set off on the return journey. Halfway back, though, he was overcome by an irresistible desire to sleep. He set the jug down on the ground and fell fast asleep. By now the Tsar was already dressing for dinner. The servants laid the table and brought fresh-baked bread and sweet honeys. But Fleet-of-Foot slept on and on.

Marksman spotted him and shot a red-hot arrow right at his forehead. Fleet-of-Foot woke up, untied his second leg, snatched up the jug and reached the palace just in time — as the Tsar was entering the dining-room.

So Vaniushka had accomplished all the tasks, but still the Tsar did not want to let him have the princess.

"Take as much gold and as many pearls," he told him, "as one man can carry and be gone. Fly away out of my realm!"

They sewed a huge sack and filled it with gold. The Tsar thought to himself: "No-one can possibly lift that amount," but Strongman swung the sack onto his back and carried it onto the ship.

The Tsar regretted the loss of his treasure and he sent his soldiers after Vaniushka. They fired cannon at the ship and threatened to kill Vaniushka.

Vaniushka was filled with alarm:

"Now I am lost for certain! Where can I find an army?"

The man with the bundle of firewood stepped forward:

"Well, you are forgetful! What about me?"

He climbed out into the field and scattered his bundle of firewood. Immediately an army too large to count sprang up — horsemen, foot-soldiers and cannon. They began to rout the Tsar's forces.

At this the Tsar was terrified and he decided: "Better to be on good terms with him, or he will take the whole of my kingdom."

And he called off his men.

Then all nine companions boarded the flying ship and they sailed across the great sea to the wonderful island of Buyan.

And they are living there to this day.

Sister Alionushka and Brother Ivanushka

Once upon a time there lived an old man and woman who had a daughter named Aliónushka and a young son named Ivánushka.

The old couple died and Alionushka and Ivanushka were left alone, without anybody in the whole world.

Alionushka went out to work and took her brother with her. They walked a long way through the fields and Ivanushka grew thirsty.

"Sister Alionushka, I want to drink!"

"Wait, little brother, until we get to the well."

They walked and walked. The sun stood high in the sky; the well was still far off, and the heat was oppressive. They came to a cattle trough full of water.

"Sister Alionushka, let me take a sip from the trough!"

"Don't drink, little brother, or you'll turn into a calf."

Ivanushka obeyed her and they walked on.

The sun stood high in the sky; the well was still far off, and the heat was oppressive. They came to a horse trough full of water.

"Sister Alionushka, let me take a sip from the trough!"

"Don't drink, little brother, or you'll turn into a foal."

Ivanushka sighed, and they walked on again.

They walked and walked. The sun stood high in the sky; the well was still far off, and the heat was oppressive. They came to a goat trough full of water.

Ivanushka said:

"Sister Alionushka, I can't go on: I must drink from this trough!"

"Don't drink, little brother, or you'll turn into a kid."

Ivanushka did not listen and drank his fill from the trough.

He slaked his thirst and … turned into a kid!

Alionushka called to her brother and instead of Ivanushka a little white goat came running after her.

Alionushka burst into tears. She sat down under a haystack to cry, and the kid gambolled around her.

Just then a merchant drove by in his cart.

"Why are you crying, beautiful maiden?"

Alionushka told him of her misfortune.

The merchant said:

"Well, why don't you marry me. I'll dress you in gold and silver, and the little goat will live with us."

Alionushka thought and thought and agreed to marry the merchant.

She moved into his house and they all lived together. The goat ate and drank with them.

Once, when the merchant was away, a witch appeared from out of nowhere. She stood under Alionushka's window and called her to come and bathe in the river.

She was so persuasive that Alionushka went down to the river with her. When they got there, she seized Alionushka, fastened a stone round her neck and threw her into the water.

Then the witch made herself the very spit and image of Alionushka, dressed in her clothes and went into her house. Nobody noticed the change. Even the merchant when he came back believed she was Alionushka.

Only the little goat knew the truth. He pined away, refusing to eat or drink. Morning and evening he went down to the river bank and called out:

"Alionushka, sister dear!
Come out of the river and back to me here…"

The witch found out and began asking her husband to slaughter the kid.

The merchant felt sorry for the little goat as he had grown very fond of him, but the witch nagged so much that at last he agreed.

The witch ordered the servants to build fires in the yard, to heat the iron vessels and to sharpen the knives.

The goat realised that he did not have long to live and said to his foster-father:

"Before I die, let me go down to the river and drink some water. It will clean out my insides."

"Very well, off you go."

The little goat ran down to the river, stood on the bank and called out in a plaintive voice:

"Alionushka, sister dear!
Come out of the river and back to me here...
The fires are a-burning
The vessels a-boiling
The knives a-sharpening.
They're going to slit my throat!"

And from the river Alionushka answered him:

"O, little brother, Ivanushka!
A heavy stone weighs me down.
The weeds have twined around my legs.
How hard it is to drown!"

By now the witch was looking for the little goat and sent a servant down to the river:
"Go and find the little goat and bring him back to me."

The servant went down to the river and saw the little goat running up and down the bank and calling out in a plaintive voice:

"Alionushka, sister dear!
Come out of the river and back to me here...
The fires are a-burning
The vessels a-boiling
The knives a-sharpening.
They're going to slit my throat!"

And from the river the answer came:

"O, little brother, Ivanushka!
A heavy stone weighs me down.
The weeds have twined around my legs.
How hard it is to drown!"

The servant hurried back to the house and told the merchant what he had heard. They got a party together, went down and dragged the river. They found Alionushka and pulled her out. They untied the stone from her neck, plunged her in spring water and dressed her in a fine dress. Alionushka came back to life and became more beautiful than before.

The little goat was so delighted that he jumped head-over-heels three times and turned back into a boy.

They seized the witch, tied her to a horse's tail and drove her out into the steppe.

Morozko

There was once a peasant who lived with his second wife. He had one daughter and so did his wife.

Everyone knows what it is like to live with a step-mother: do something too much and you are beaten, don't do it enough and you are beaten. Yet her own daughter, whatever she does, gets stroked on the head and called a good girl.

The step-daughter fed and water the animals, brought firewood and water into the house, fed the stove and swept out the house — all before it was light. Yet nothing pleased the woman — everything was done wrong.

The wind might make a row for a time, but then it falls silent, while an old woman when she gets worked up can go on and on. The step-mother eventually decided to be rid of the girl altogether.

"Take her out in the sledge," she told her husband, "wherever you want so that I no longer have to look at her! Take her to the forest and leave her in the freezing cold!"

The old man was grief-stricken and his eyes filled with tears, but she nagged so much he had to agree. He harnessed the horse to the sledge and said:

"Come, daughter dear, and ride in the sledge."

He took the unfortunate girl into the forest, tipped her into a snow-drift beneath a huge fir-tree and hurried away.

The girl sat beneath the fir and shivered. Soon she was shaking from head to foot. Suddenly she heard Morózko — which is what the Russians call Jack Frost — nearby, making his way through the firs, leaping from tree to tree snapping and cracking. He sprang onto the top of the fir beneath which the girl was sitting and called down to her:

"Are you warm, my girl?"

"Quite warm, dear Morozko, quite warm."

Morozko started to come down the tree and the snapping and cracking grew stronger:

"Are you warm, my girl? Are you warm, my beauty?"

"Quite warm, dear Morozko, quite warm."

She could hardly get the words out.

Morozko came lower still, snapping and cracking all the more:

"Are you warm, my girl? Are you warm, my beauty? Are you warm, my sweet?"

The girl was frozen to the bone. She could barely move her tongue:

"Oh, quite warm, Morozko, my darling!"

At that Morozko took pity on the girl, wrapped her in warm furs, and warmed her with quilted blankets.

Meanwhile the step-mother was preparing for her wake, cooking pancakes, as is the Russian tradition. She called out to her husband:

"Go on then, you old fool, bring your daughter back for burial!"

The old man went off to the forest and when he got to the spot where he had left her he found his daughter sitting there ruddy-cheeked and happy. She was wearing a sable coat and gold and silver from head to foot, while a chest of rich presents lay next to her.

The old man was overjoyed, loaded everything into the sledge, sat his daughter alongside him and headed for home.

Meanwhile the old woman was still cooking pancakes, when from under the table the dog barked out:

"Woof, woof! The old man's daughter will come in silver and gold; the old woman's daughter will leave suitors cold."

The woman tossed him a pancake:

"That's the wrong words. You should say: 'The old woman's daughter will have suitors by the score; the old man's daughter lives no more.'"

The dog ate the pancake and repeated:

"Woof, woof! The old man's daughter will come in silver and gold, the old woman's daughter will leave suitors cold."

The old woman tried giving him pancakes and beating him, but the dog would not change his tune...

Suddenly the gates creaked, the door flew open and her step-daughter came in, decked in gold and silver, looking simply radiant. Behind her the old man carried the large, heavy chest. The old woman stared and threw up her arms...

"Quick, you old fool, harness the other horse to the sledge! Take my daughter into the forest and leave her in the same place."

The man put his wife's daughter in the sledge, took her into the forest, tipped her into the same snow-drift beneath the huge fir and hurried away.

The old woman's daughter sat and her teeth began chattering.

Then Morozko came leaping through the forest from tree to tree, snapping and cracking. He looked down at the old woman's daughter:

"Are you warm, my girl?"

"Icy cold. Don't snap, Morozko! Don't crack!"

Morozko started to come down the tree and the snapping and cracking grew stronger:

"Are you warm, my girl? Are you warm, my beauty?"

"I can't feel my hands and feet. Go away, Morozko!"

Morozko came lower still, snapping and cracking all the more:

"Are you warm, my girl? Are you warm, my beauty? Are you warm, my sweet?"

"Simply frozen! Be off with you, Morozko, you fiend!"

At that Morozko lost his temper, and seized the girl so that she turned to ice.

As soon as it was light the old woman sent her husband off:

"Harness the sledge quickly, you old fool, and fetch my daughter back decked in gold and silver."

The old man left and from under the table the dog barked out:

"Woof, woof! The old man's daughter will have suitors by the score; the old woman's daughter lives no more."

The woman threw him a pie:

"That's the wrong words. You should say 'The old woman's daughter will come in silver and gold...'"

But the dog would not change his tune:

"Woof, woof! The old man's daughter will have suitors by the score..."

Suddenly the gates creaked, the old woman rushed to greet her daughter. She turned back the blanket, and there was her daughter dead in the sledge.

The old woman howled and wailed, but it was too late.

Nikita the Tanner

Russian people lived in the city of Kiev. They built houses, laid out their gardens, tilled the soil and sang songs.

All of a sudden from lands unknown Gorýnych the dragon came to Kiev. His body was green, his eyes red, his wings were made of iron, his claws of bronze. Ten heads and ten trunks were attached to snake-like necks.

The dragon roared and hissed so powerfully that the leaves flew from the trees.

"I shall burn this city of Kiev, I shall slay all the people, I shall dig up all the earth. If you want to remain alive, then every month give me a beautiful maiden — a meal for me, salvation for you!"

What could they do? How can you fight against such a monster? The people groaned and wept, but there was nothing for it but to give Gorynych the dragon a maiden each month.

They took the beautiful girl to the top of a tall hill and attached her to an oak with chains. Gorynych tore the century-old oak out by the roots, carried it away to his lair, snapped the chains and devoured the maiden.

Before very long he had devoured all the maidens in the city. Only the Tsar's daughter remained. The time came when she had to go and be eaten by the dragon.

The Tsar wept, the Tsarina howled. The city was hung with black flags and the whole country groaned.

They took the princess to the tall hill and fastened her to an oak with chains of gold. There she stood, more dead than alive. Her light brown plait had come loose and hung down to her knees. Then Gorynych came flying down. He saw her incomparable beauty and forgot about eating her. He tore the chains from her, sat her on one iron wing and carried her off to his lair.

"You will stay here," he told her, "and keep house for me."

She found the idea even worse than death.

One day passed, and a second day dawned.

The dragon wanted to go about his business and so he sealed the princess up inside the cave with century-old oaks, so that she could not get away. He wove the branches and twisted the trunks together so that no man could pass through, nor even a beast.

In her room at the palace the princess had kept a grey-winged, blue-breasted dove. Now he went flying over the woods and fields, constantly seeking his lost mistress. He passed the dragon's lair just as the princess was singing a sad song. On hearing her voice, the dove flew to the cave, found a tiny gap between the green branches and squeezed through into the dragon's lair. He had crumpled his wing a little, but he reached the princess. How pleased she was to see him! She talked and talked. She asked about everything — how were her mother and father, what was happening in Kiev, were the flowers blooming in the meadows, was the corn growing in the fields, were the larks singing in the sky? You see, in that dark cave she could not see or hear anything — the breeze did not reach her; the sun did not warm her. The dove told here everything she wanted to know and as evening approached he flew away.

He began to come every day, bringing the princess news from the Tsar and Tsarina, and telling her everything that was going on in the world.

Then one day the dove said:

"Your father, the Tsar, asks you to try to find out from the dragon whether there is anything in the world more powerful than him."

In the evening the dragon flew back and tossed aside the century-old oaks at the mouth of the cave. Their thick branches snapped like threads, their trunks bent like straws.

And the princess said to him:

"Oh, how strong you are, Gorynych! There is probably nothing in the world stronger than you!"

The dragon replied:

"In Kiev there is a man stronger than me — Nikita the Tanner who lives in the Leather-Workers' settlement. If Nikita starts to stoke the stove the smoke rises up to the clouds; if Nikita goes down to the Dnieper to soak ox-hides he carries not one, but a dozen at once. When the hides had swollen with water, I went up and fastened on to them. Well, I thought, now he won't be able to pull the hides out of the river — they have become awfully heavy. And he didn't care… rolls up his sleeves, plants his feet apart and very nearly pulls me up onto the bank. There you are — Nikita the Tanner is the one thing in the world that I fear."

The princess made no response to what the dragon said, as if she had not been listening.

The next day, when the dove came, she said to him:

"My grey-winged, blue-breasted dove, tell my father, the Tsar, that Nikita the Tanner who lives in the Leather-Workers' settlement in Kiev is stronger than Gorynych the dragon."

When the Tsar heard about Nikita the Tanner, he went himself to the Leather Workers' settlement.

Nikita was busy kneading hides. When he caught sight of the Tsar, he began to tremble with fright. His hands shook and he tore a dozen ox-hides into little pieces, leaving nothing but thin strips.

The Tsar saw that and was astonished. He had never heard of such strength.

"Well, Nikita the Tanner," the Tsar said, "you certainly are strong. You alone can deal with the dragon. Deliver the world from Gorynych the dragon, and save my daughter the Princess Maryushka."

Nikita the Tanner just stood and shook, his knees growing weak with fear.

"But, Your Majesty," he said, "I am a timid man, how am I to deal with the dragon?"

The Tsar tried everything he could think of to persuade him — silver, gold, the finest pearls — but Nikita remained as reluctant as ever.

The Tsar then gathered together five thousand small children.

They went down on their knees in front of Nikita, crying, wailing, and pouring out tears:

"Have pity on us, dear Nikita: a few years will pass and we too will all go to be eaten by the accursed dragon. Have pity on us, rescue us, Nikita!"

Nikita had pity on them and gave his consent.

And so he began to prepare for the battle.

Nikita took three hundred *poods* of hemp, soaked it in pitch and wrapped himself in it from head to foot. Then he covered himself with ox-hides and went out to meet Gorynych.

The dragon heard that Nikita was coming and sealed himself up in his lair. He set about sharpening his teeth and pointing his claws.

Nikita shouted in a loud voice:

"Come out in the open, monster, and fight honestly, otherwise I shall destroy your lair and kill you where you hide!"

With that he began slashing at the century-old oaks with such force that they broke into splinters.

The dragon sprang out of its cave and they began to fight. The very earth trembled and the trees shook from the roots.

The dragon lunged and grabbed Nikita in his teeth. He tore off a piece of ox-hide and his teeth caught in the pitch-soaked hemp, but Nikita was unhurt.

Nikita hit the dragon with a great club that weighed fully ten *poods*. With every blow the creature sank further into the ground. He struck again and again until Gorynych rolled on the ground and he planted his foot on him.

Then the dragon began to whimper and begged:

"Do not beat me to death, Nikita the Tanner. There is no-one stronger than us in the whole world. Let us divide up the whole Earth equally between us — you rule in one half and I shall live out my days in the other."

"Very well," the tanner said, "but there must be a boundary line drawn between us."

Nikita forged a plough weighing three hundred *poods*, harnessed the dragon to it and started to plough a furrow from Kiev. The dragon pulled the plough, panting and puffing, while Nikita rode on top, driving the dragon on with a switch:

"Hey, Gorynych, keep the furrow straight!"

So Nikita the Tanner drew his boundary line from Kiev to the Caspian Sea.

"Well," the dragon said, "now you and I have divided up the whole Earth."

"We've divided the earth," Nikita said. "Now let's divide the sea. Otherwise you'll be saying that I am taking your water, or soaking my skins in it."

Nikita drove the dragon out into the Caspian Sea.

The three-hundred-*pood* plough was dragging Gorynych to the bottom and Nikita the Tanner helped him on his way with blows from his iron club, saying:

"Keep the furrow straight, dragon. Plough the water deeper."

Gorynych the dragon struggled and struggled, and finally drowned in the middle of the sea.

Afterwards Nikita dragged his body to the shore, so that the monster would not spoil the water.

He built a fire and burnt the dragon, scattering the ashes to the winds. That was a mistake — he should have buried the ashes, for as soon as the wind caught them they turned into flies, mosquitoes, midges and other creatures that trouble people in summer to this day. And off they went humming and buzzing around the world.

If Nikita had only buried the ashes in the ground, we would have been spared all that discomfort.

Anyway, that is how Nikita the Tanner delivered the Russian land from the dragon. He broke down the monster's lair, released the princess and took her back to her mother and father. The Tsar and Tsarina wept for joy. Throughout Kiev people rejoiced, sang and praised Nikita. They brought the tanner silver, gold, the finest pearls, expensive clothes and good things to eat.

Nikita wanted none of it. He only took a crust of bread and an onion and went back to the Leather Workers' settlement to knead his ox-hides.

The Swan-Geese

A peasant man lived with his wife in a village. They had a daughter and a son who was still quite small.

One day the mother said: "Daughter, we are going to work now. Look after your little brother. Don't leave the yard and if you are a good girl we will buy you a shawl."

The mother and father went off and soon the girl forgot what she had been told. She sat her little brother down on the grass in the yard, and went out into the street where she got so involved in a game that she wandered farther and farther from home.

Meanwhile the swan-geese came flying by, seized the boy and carried him off with them.

At last the girl came back, only to find her brother gone. She groaned and dashed about, looking everywhere. She called him, cried and warned what would happen when their parents returned, but the boy did not appear.

She ran out into the open country and then, way off in the distance, she spotted the swan-geese just as they disappeared behind the dark forest. She guessed that they must have taken her brother away. It had long been said that the swan-geese were fond of such tricks as carrying off little children.

The girl went chasing after them. She ran and ran until she came to a stove.

"Stove, o stove, tell me where the swan-geese have flown."

The stove replied: "Eat some of my rye cake and I shall tell you."

"I'll not eat rye cakes. In my father's house we do not even eat wheat cakes."

The stove did not tell her. The girl ran on until she came to an apple-tree.

"Apple-tree, o apple-tree, tell me where the swan-geese have flown."

"Eat my crab apples and I shall tell you."

"In my father's house we do not even eat apples from the orchard."

The apple-tree did not tell her. The girl ran on until she came to a river of milk flowing through banks of *kissél*, which is a kind of starchy jelly.

"O river of milk, o banks of *kissel*, tell me where the swan-geese have flown."

"Eat my plain *kissel* with milk and I shall tell you."

"In my father's house we do not even eat cream."

She ran on for a long way, through fields and woods. The daylight was beginning to fade and soon she would have no choice but to turn for home. Then suddenly she saw a hut standing on chicken legs. It had a single window and was turning round in circles.

Inside the old witch Bába-Yagá sat spinning flax. And on the bench there sat her brother playing with silver apples. The girl went into the hut.

"Good evening."

"Good evening, girl. Why have you come here?"

"I have been walking in the moss, over the marshes. My dress is wet and I came to get warm."

"Sit down then and spin for a while."

Baba-Yaga gave her the spindle and went outside. The girl started spinning and suddenly a little mouse popped out from under the stove and said:

"Girl, give me some porridge and I will tell you something you should know."

The girl gave the mouse some porridge and it said:

"Baba-Yaga has gone to stoke the fire in the bathhouse. She'll wash you clean then put you in the oven, roast you and eat you. Later she will roll around on your bones."

The girl sat frozen to the spot with tears running down her cheeks. The mouse went on:

"Don't wait. Take your brother and run. I shall spin the flax for you."

The girl grabbed her brother and ran. Baba-Yaga came up to the window of the hut and called inside: "Girl, are you spinning?"

"Yes, I am," the mouse replied.

Baba-Yaga finished heating the bathhouse and went to fetch the girl. But there was no-one in the hut. Baba-Yaga shouted out:

"Swan-Geese, after them! The girl has carried her brother off!"

Brother and sister ran to the river of milk. Then the girl spotted the swan-geese flying after them.

"River, dear river, hide me!"

"Eat my plain *kissel*."

The girl ate it and said thank you. The river hid her under its banks of *kissel*. The swan-geese could not see the girl and flew on by. The girl and her brother continued running, but the swan-geese turned round and came flying back towards them. Any minute now they would spot them. There was nothing left to hope for, and then they came to the apple-tree.

"Apple-tree, dear apple-tree, hide me!"

"Eat my crab apples."

The girl ate as quickly as she could and said thank you. The apple-tree wrapped her in its branches and covered her with its leaves. The swan-geese could not see the girl and flew on by. The girl ran on again. She ran and ran, and, when there was only a little way to go, the swan-geese spotted her. They cackled loudly, beat the air with their wings and were on the point of snatching the boy from his sister's arms when she reached the stove.

"Stove, dear stove, hide me!"

"Eat some of my rye cake."

The girl popped the cake into her mouth as quick as she could, then climbed into the stove with her brother, and sat where the fire would be. The swan-geese dived and circled, honked and screeched, but in the end they had to admit defeat and fly back to Baba-Yaga.

The girl thanked the stove and ran home with her brother. Just as they reached the house, their mother and father came back.

The Wooden Eagle

Once upon a time, in a certain kingdom, there was a Tsar who had a great many servants. Now those servants were not ordinary lackeys, but craftsmen of various kinds: cabinet-makers, potters, tailors and more. The Tsar liked to have clothes that were cut better than the rest, dishes that were painted with more striking designs and a palace that was adorned with intricate carving.

There were so many craftsmen in the royal palace that you could not even count them. In the morning they used to gather outside the Tsar's private apartments and wait for him to come out and give his orders for the day.

On one occasion a goldsmith and a carpenter bumped into each other on the very threshold of the royal apartments. They immediately began arguing over which of them knew his own craft better and whose trade was the more difficult.

The goldsmith said:

"Your craft is no great thing. You simply carve things out of wood. But look at my work: I make everything out of pure gold that's a real feast for the eyes."

The carpenter countered:

"It's not clever to make a precious thing, when gold itself is so costly. You try turning ordinary wood into something that will amaze everyone who sees it. Then I shall believe that you are a master."

The argument went on and on, and might have turned into a fight, if the Tsar had not chosen that moment to appear. He had heard their talk and, grinning to himself, gave his orders:

"Each of you should make me a wonder: one of gold, the other of wood. I shall inspect them and decide which of you is the better craftsman."

You do not argue with a tsar if you value your life. The craftsmen went back to their workshops, each thinking hard how to outdo the other in a display of skill. The Tsar gave them a week for the task.

In a week both craftsmen came back to the palace, took their places with the others and waited for the Tsar to appear. Each of them held a bundle in his arms.

The Tsar came out and said:

"Well, my fine fellows, are you ready to demonstrate your skills," and laughed into his beard.

He sent servants to fetch the Tsarina and the Tsarevich, their son who was then a young man.

"Let them see your work as well."

The Tsar and Tsarina sat down on a bench and the Tsarevich stood alongside them. The goldsmith came forward:

"Be so kind, Your Majesty, as to have a large tub of water brought."

Servants brought in a large tub and filled it with water.

The goldsmith unwrapped his bundle and took out a gold duck that he placed on the water. The duck swam as if it was alive, turned its head, quacked and preened its feathers with its beak.

The Tsar's mouth fell open with astonishment, but the Tsarina shouted:

"That's a real duck, not a golden one! He must have covered a real duck with gold leaf."

The goldsmith was offended:

"What do you mean a real duck! If you allow me, I shall take it apart and put it back together."

He took the duck out of the tub and unscrewed first its wings, then its head, then took it all to pieces. He spread them all out on a table, then set about putting them together again.

He fastened the last screw and returned the duck to the water. It swam even better than before.

All the courtiers clapped:

"What a craftsman! What a wonder! I've not seen anything like it in my life!"

The Tsar turned to the carpenter:

"Now you show your skills."

The carpenter bowed:

"Be so kind, Your Majesty, as to have the window of this chamber opened wide."

The window was opened. The carpenter unwrapped his bundle and took out a wooden eagle. The bird was so finely made that it could not be distinguished from a real one. And the carpenter announced:

"That golden duck can swim, but my eagle will soar into the clouds."

The carpenter sat on the eagle and turned a small screw. The eagle lifted him up and in an instant flew out of the room. Everyone dashed to the window to see the carpenter performing various tricks in the air above the courtyard. He turned the little screw to the left and the eagle dropped down, he turned it to the right and it rose. The Tsar was so astonished his crown slipped to the back of his head, but he kept staring out of the window, unable to tear his eyes away. In fact everyone was rooted to the spot — they had never seen such craftsmanship.

The carpenter performed a final circle and flew back into the room. He set the eagle on one side and approached the Tsar.

"Well, Your Majesty, are you satisfied with my skills?"

"I cannot find the words to express my satisfaction," the Tsar replied. "How did you manage to do it? And how did you fit it with that little screw?"

The carpenter had begun to explain to the Tsar, when suddenly the Tsarina shouted out:

"Hey! Where are you going? Quick, stop him! Catch him!"

Everyone span round to see that while the Tsar had been questioning the carpenter, the young Tsarevich had leapt onto the eagle, turned the screw and flown out of the window into the courtyard.

"Come back right now! Where are you going! You'll kill yourself!" the Tsar and Tsarina shouted after him.

But the Tsarevich waved his hand and flew on over the silver railings that surrounded the palace. He turned the little screw to the right and the eagle rose into the clouds and was lost from sight.

The Tsarina collapsed, but the Tsar vented his anger on the carpenter.

"You deliberately invented such a thing," he said, "so as to deprive us of our only son. Guards! Take this man and throw him into the dungeon. If the Tsarevich does not come back within two weeks, the carpenter goes to the gallows."

The guards seized the carpenter and threw him into a dark dungeon. Meanwhile the Tsarevich flew further and further on the wooden eagle.

He was enjoying himself — the wide open space all around, the wind whistling in his ears and blowing out his curls, the clouds flitting past beneath his feet. The Tsarevich felt like a bird himself.

He turned this way and that, wherever the fancy took him.

By evening he had reached an unknown kingdom and brought the eagle down on the edge of a town. He looked around and saw a small house.

The Tsarevich knocked on the door and an old woman appeared.

"Let me in, good woman, to spend the night. I am a stranger here and have nowhere to stay."

"Come on in, son. Why not? I live alone and have plenty of room."

The Tsarevich dismantled the eagle, wrapped it up and stepped into the house.

The old woman gave him supper and the Tsarevich asked about the town, who lived there and what wonders might be seen there.

And the old woman replied:

"There is one wonder in this kingdom of ours, son. In the middle of the town stands the royal palace and alongside the palace is a tall tower. The tower is closed up with thirty locks and thirty men guard its gates. No-one is allowed into the tower and the Tsar's daughter lives there. As soon as she was born, she and her nurse were locked up in that tower, so that no-one might see her. The Tsar and Tsarina are afraid that the princess will fall in love with someone and they will have to let her marry and go abroad. They are afraid to part with her, as she is their only child. So the girl lives in the tower, as if in prison."

"And is she really beautiful?" the Tsarevich asked.

"That I cannot tell, son, for I have not seen her myself, but they do say that for fairness she has no like in the whole wide world."

The Tsarevich immediately wanted to get inside the forbidden tower. He lay down to sleep and pondered over how he could catch a glimpse of the princess.

The next day, as darkness fell, he mounted his wooden eagle, soared into the clouds and approached the tower from the side where there was a window.

He flew up and tapped on the glass.

The princess was astonished to see a young man more handsome than can be described.

"Who are you, young sir?" she asked.

"Open the window and I shall tell you everything."

The girl opened the window and the wooden eagle flew into the room. The Tsarevich climbed off, greeted the girl and told her who he was and how he came to be there.

They sat down and looked at each other, unable to tear their eyes away.

The Tsarevich asked if she was willing to become his wife.

"I myself am willing," the princess said, "but I fear my father and mother will not let me go."

The wicked nurse who guarded the princess saw and heard everything. She ran to the palace and told the whole story — some young man had flown into the princess's room and now he was hiding in the house of the old woman.

The guards hurried to the house, seized the Tsarevich and dragged him to the palace. The Tsar sat on his throne banging his staff on the floor in fury:

"How dare you, you rogue, go against my royal command. I shall have you executed tomorrow!"

They took the Tsarevich to the dungeon, left him there alone and closed it up with strong locks.

In the morning all the townspeople were made to gather in the square. It was proclaimed that a bold young man was to be executed for entering the princess's tower.

The hangman came and set up the gallows and the Tsar and Tsarina themselves arrived to watch the execution.

The Tsarevich was brought out. He turned to the Tsar and said:

"Your Majesty, permit me one final request."

The Tsar frowned, but he could not refuse:

"Well, speak up."

"Send a messenger to the house of the old woman, where I was living, to fetch my bundle."

The Tsar could not refuse and sent a messenger who returned with the bundle.

By that time the Tsarevich had already been brought to the gallows and was standing on the steps. The messenger handed him the bundle.

The Tsarevich unwrapped it, mounted the wooden eagle — and was off. He soared above the gallows, the Tsar and the whole crowd.

The Tsar groaned:

"Catch him! Hold him! He'll get away!"

But the Tsarevich turned the eagle towards the tower, flew up to the window, seized the princess and sat her on the eagle in front of him.

"Well," he said, "now you and I need have no fear of pursuit."

And the eagle carried them back to the Tsarevich's homeland. There the unfortunate carpenter sat in his dungeon, his eyes glued to the small window, scanning the sky for the Tsarevich coming back. The two weeks were to end the next day and the carpenter would hang unless the Tsarevich returned.

Suddenly he spotted the wooden eagle flying through the air, and, mounted upon it, not just the Tsarevich but a beautiful maiden as well.

      The eagle landed in the middle of the palace courtyard. The Tsarevich helped his bride off and brought her to his father and mother. He told them where he had been for two weeks. In their joy they forgave him the alarm he had caused them and had the carpenter released from the dungeon.

      The Tsar held a great feast and the wedding celebrations went on for three months.

Khavroshechka

There are in this world good people, people who are not so bad and those who simply have no shame.

It was among this last sort that Little Khavróshechka found herself after her parents died. She was taken in by a woman who brought her up and set her to work all the hours that God sent: she wove and span as well as cleaning and tidying and being responsible for the whole household.

Now her mistress had three daughters. The eldest was called One-Eye, the second Two-Eyes and the third Three-Eyes.

Those daughters had nothing better to do than to sit by the gate and watch what happened in the street, while Little Khavroshechka did all the work for them: sewed all their clothes, span and wove for them — and never heard a kind word from anybody.

When she felt really sad, Little Khavroshechka went out into the field and threw her arms around the neck of the family's piebald cow, pressed herself to its warm side and poured her heart out:

"O dear cow. They beat and scold me, don't give me bread and tell me not to cry. By tomorrow I am supposed to spin and weave five *poods* of flax, bleach the linen and roll it all up."

The cow replied:

"My beautiful girl, climb into one of my ears and out of the other and everything will be done."

And that is just how it was: Khavroshechka climbed into one of the cow's ears and out of the other and everything was ready. The flax had been woven and bleached and now lay in rolls.

She carried the linen in to her mistress. The woman looked, grunted and hid it away in a chest. Then she gave Little Khavroshechka even more work to do.

Again the unfortunate girl went out to the cow, hugged and stroked it, climbed in one ear and out of the other. She gratefully took up the finished work and carried it to her mistress.

This time the woman called her daughter One-Eye and said to her:

"Good daughter, lovely daughter, go and look who is helping the orphan; who is spinning and weaving and rolling the linen."

One-Eye followed Khavroshechka into the forest and out again into the field, but it was a warm day. She forgot her mother's orders, lay down on the grass and soaked up the sun.

Khavroshechka whispered:

"Sleep, little eye. Sleep, little eye."

And One-Eye's eye dozed off. While One-Eye was asleep, the cow wove and bleached and rolled the linen.

So the mistress learnt nothing and decided to send her second daughter, Two-Eyes:

"Good daughter, lovely daughter, go and look who is helping the orphan; who is spinning and weaving and rolling the linen."

Two-Eyes followed Khavroshechka, but it was a warm day. She forgot her mother's orders, lay down on the grass and soaked up the sun.

Khavroshechka whispered:

"Sleep, one little eye. Sleep, two little eyes."

And Two-Eyes' eyes dozed off. The cow wove and bleached and rolled the linen, and Two-Eyes kept on sleeping.

The old woman grew angry and on the third day she sent her youngest daughter, Three-Eyes, and gave the poor orphan even more work to do.

Three-Eyes danced and skipped about, grew warm in the sun and lay down on the grass.

Khavroshechka whispered:

"Sleep, one little eye. Sleep, two little eyes."

But she forgot about the third eye. Two of Three-Eyes' eyes did doze off, but one stayed awake and watched all that happened. It saw Khavroshechka climb in one of the cow's ears and out of the other and then pick up the finished linen.

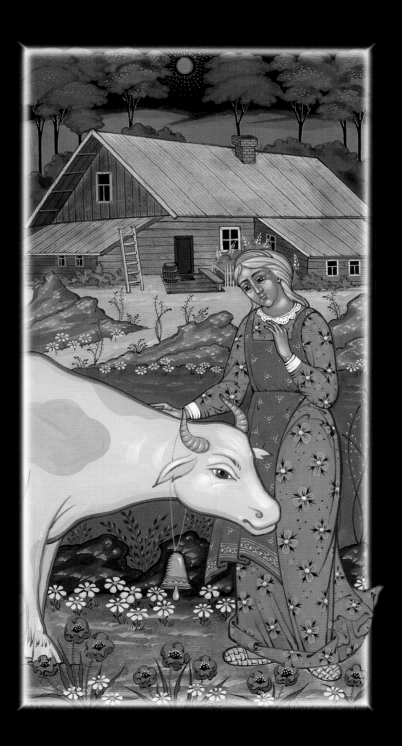

Three-Eyes went back home and told her mother all about it.

The spiteful woman was delighted and the next day she began nagging her husband to slaughter the piebald cow.

The old man tried to argue with her:

"Have you gone mad? The cow is still young and a good milker."

"Slaughter it, and be quick about it!"

She would not budge and the old man began sharpening the knife. Khavroshechka found out, ran into the field, hugged the piebald cow and said:

"Dear cow, they are going to kill you."

And the cow replied:

"Then you, my beautiful girl, should not eat my meat, but collect my bones, wrap them in a cloth, bury them in the garden and never forget me. Go out and water the bones every morning."

The old man slaughtered the cow and Khavroshechka followed the animal's instructions faithfully. Though she was tormented by hunger, she never ate its meat. She buried its bones and watered them in the garden every day.

And from the bones a wonderful apple-tree sprang up — with ripe juicy apples, golden leaves and heavy silver branches. Anyone who rode stopped to look, and those who came close simply stood and stared.

One day the three sisters, One-Eye, Two-Eyes and Three-Eyes, were strolling in the garden when a fine figure of a man rode by — rich, young and curly-haired. He saw the lovely juicy apples in the garden and he called out to the sisters:

"My fine young ladies, I have decided to marry whichever of you brings me one of those apples!"

The sisters rushed to be first to the tree.

The apples had been hanging low, where they were easy to reach, but now they suddenly sprang up high above the girls' heads.

The sisters tried to knock them down, but the leaves got in their eyes. They tried to pull off the branches, but they tied themselves in knots. They struggled and strained, but they got nothing more than skinned hands for their pains.

Then Khavroshechka went up to the tree. The branches bowed down to her and the apples put themselves into her hands. She offered the best one to the young man and he took her away to be his wife. From that time on she lived happily and never knew any more sorrow.

Sivka-Burka

There was once an old man who had three sons. The elder two looked after the farm. They were well-to-do and were fond of putting on airs, but the youngest, known as Ivan the Fool, was nothing much to look at and liked to go gathering mushrooms in the forest, while at home he spent most of his time sitting in the warm on the stove.

The time came for the old man to die and he told his sons:

"When I have gone, you should come to my grave three nights in succession and bring me bread."

They buried the old man. When night came, the eldest brother was supposed to go to the grave, but perhaps out of laziness, perhaps out of fear, he did not feel like it and said to the youngest:

"Vanya, take my place tonight. Go to father's grave and I'll buy you some spice-cake."

Ivan agreed, took some bread and went to his father's grave. There he sat and waited. At midnight the earth opened, his father rose up out of the grave and asked:

"Who's there? Is it you, my eldest son? Tell me what is happening in Russia: are the dogs a-barking, the wolves a-howling, or my children a-crying?"

Ivan replied: "It is me, your son. And in Russia all is well."

The father ate his fill of bread and lay back in the grave.

Ivan headed for home, collecting mushrooms on the way. When he got back, the eldest brother asked him:

"Did you see father?"

"Yes, I did."

"Did he eat the bread."

"Yes, he ate his fill."

The second night came round. It was the middle brother's turn to go, but perhaps out of laziness, perhaps out of fear, he did not feel like it and said to the youngest:

"Vanya, go to father's grave for me and I'll make you a pair of bast shoes."

"All right."

Ivan took some bread, went to his father's grave, sat and waited.

At midnight the earth opened, his father rose up out of the grave and asked:

"Who's there? Is it you, my middle son? Tell me what is happening in Russia: are the dogs a-barking, the wolves a-howling, or my children a-crying?"

Ivan replied: "It is me, your son. And in Russia all is well."

The father ate his fill of bread and lay back in the grave.

Ivan headed for home, collecting mushrooms again on the way. When he got back, the middle brother asked him:

"Did father eat the bread."

"Yes, he ate his fill."

On the third night it was Ivan's own turn to go. He said to his brothers:

"I have been for two nights now. You go to father's grave this time and I shall have a rest."

But his brothers answered:

"No, no, Vanya. You know what it's like already, you'd better go."

"Very well then."

Ivan took some bread and went. At midnight the earth opened, his father rose up out of the grave and asked:

"Who's there? Is it you, my youngest son? Tell me what is happening in Russia: are the dogs a-barking, the wolves a-howling, or my children a-crying?"

Ivan replied: "It is me, your son, Vanya. And in Russia all is well."

The father ate his fill of bread, then held out a bridle and said to him:

"You alone have carried out my instructions, were not afraid to come to my grave. Go out into the open country and shout: 'Sivka-Burka, wonder-worker, appear before me, like a leaf before a tree!' A horse will come running to you. You climb into its right ear and out of the left and you'll become a very fine young man. Get on the horse and go for a ride."

Ivan took the bridle, thanked his father and went home, collecting mushrooms again on the way. At home his brothers asked him:

"Did you see father?"

"Yes, I did."

"Did he eat the bread."

"Father ate his fill and did not ask us to come again."

Just at that time the Tsar sent out the word for all fine, young unmarried men to ride to his court. His daughter, the Incomparable Beauty, had given orders for a special tall tower to be built for her with a dozen columns and a dozen tiers of logs. She was going to sit at the very top of that tower and wait to see who could reach her with a single jump of his horse and kiss her on the lips. The horseman who succeeded, no matter what his birth, would be given the Tsar's daughter's hand in marriage and half the kingdom into the bargain.

Ivan's brothers heard this news and said to each other:

"Come on, let's go and try our luck."

They fed their best horses with oats, brought them out, dressed up clean, and combed their hair. Then Ivan, who was sitting on the stove behind the chimney, called out:

"Brothers, take me with you so I can try my luck."

"You stove-loving simpleton. You'd better going into the forest for mushrooms. There's no call to make a fool of yourself in front of people."

The brothers mounted their horses, cocked their hats, whistled and whooped — then all you could see of them was a cloud of dust. Ivan took the bridle and went out into the open country. Once he was there he shouted out the words his father had taught him:

"Sivka-Burka, wonder-worker, appear before me, like a leaf before a tree!"

From out of nowhere a horse came galloping. The earth trembled; flame spurted from its nostrils and columns of smoke poured from its ears. It stopped as if rooted to the spot and asked:

"What is your command?"

Ivan stroked the horse and put the bridle on it. He climbed into its right ear and out of its left, becoming a finer fellow than can be imagined or described. He mounted the horse and rode to the Tsar's court. As Sivka-Burka ran, the earth shook beneath its hooves, mountains and valleys flew by in a trice. Ivan came to the Tsar's court and found it full of more people than you could possibly count. The Incomparable Beauty sat at the very top of the tall tower.

The Tsar came out onto the porch and announced:

"Whosoever of you fine young men shall jump on his horse up to that window and kiss my daughter on the lips shall have her hand in marriage and half the kingdom as a dowry."

Then the young fellows began to jump… but the window was so high as to be simply unreachable. Ivan's brothers had their try, and did not even get halfway up. Finally Ivan's turn came.

He urged his horse to the fore, he tore, he roared, he soared — and was only two logs short of the window. He turned around and took off again — just one log short. Again he turned, circled, fired up his steed and away — he flew like a bird past the window. He kissed the princess on her lovely lips and she struck him on the forehead with her ring, leaving her mark on him.

The whole crowd erupted:

"Hold him! Stop him!"

But Ivan was already well away. He rode out into the open country, climbed into Sivka-Burka's left ear and out of his right, again becoming Ivan the Fool. He let the horse go and made his way home on foot, collecting mushrooms as he went. He wrapped a cloth around his forehead, climbed onto the stove and lay down.

His brothers came back and told him where they had been and what they had seen.

"There were fine fellows there, but one better than the rest — flew up on his horse and kissed the princess on the lips. People saw where he came from, but no-one saw where he went."

Ivan perched behind the chimney and said:

"Well, perhaps it was me."

His brothers became angry with him:

"A fool and he's talking nonsense! Sit on the stove and eat your mushrooms."

Ivan quietly unwrapped the cloth over his forehead where the princess had struck him with her ring. The room filled with light. His brothers took fright and shouted:

"Hey, fool, what are you doing? You'll set the house on fire!"

The next day the Tsar summoned everyone to a feast, all the boyars and princes, and the common people too, rich and poor, old and young.

Ivan's brothers began getting ready for the feast. Ivan asked them to take him with them, but they replied:

"Why do you want to make a fool of yourself in public? Sit on the stove and eat your mushrooms!"

The brothers mounted their best horses and rode off; Ivan followed on foot. He came to the Tsar's feast and took a seat in a far corner. The Princess Incomparable Beauty began to go around all the guests. She carried round a bowl of mead while looking out for someone with the mark on his forehead.

She had been to everyone by the time she reached Ivan. And suddenly her heart skipped. She looked at him, covered in soot with his hair uncombed.

The Princess began questioning him:

"Whose man are you? Where are you from? Why is your forehead bandaged?"

"I hurt myself."

The Princess unbandaged his forehead and suddenly light filled the palace. She cried out: "That's my mark! Here's my future husband!"

The Tsar came up and said:

"What future husband! He's ugly and covered in soot."

Ivan said to the Tsar:

"Allow me to clean myself up."

The Tsar agreed. Ivan went out into the courtyard and shouted out the words his father had taught him:

"Sivka-Burka, wonder-worker, appear before me, like a leaf before a tree!"

From out of nowhere a horse came galloping. The earth trembled; flame spurted from its nostrils and columns of smoke poured from its ears. He climbed into its right ear and out of its left, again becoming a finer fellow than can be imagined or described. The entire crowd gasped.

After that, the discussions did not last long and the happy gathering turned into a wedding feast.

The Frog Princess

Long, long ago there was a Tsar who had three sons. When the sons had all come of age, the Tsar called them to him and said:

"My dear children, while I am still not an old man, I should like to see you married and to enjoy your children, my grandchildren."

The sons replied:

"Well then, father, give us your blessing. Tell us who our brides are to be."

"Do as I say, my sons. Each take an arrow, go out into the open countryside and shoot it. Wherever the arrow lands, that is where your destiny lies."

The sons left their father; each took an arrow and went out into the open countryside. They drew their bows and shot.

The eldest son's arrow fell into a boyar's courtyard and was picked up by the boyar's daughter. The second son's arrow fell in the courtyard of a great merchant's house and was picked up by the merchant's daughter.

The youngest son, Ivan-Tsarevich, shot his arrow. It rose into the air and flew so far that he could not see where it landed. He walked and walked and at last he came to a marsh. Sitting there was a frog holding his arrow. Ivan-Tsarevich called:

"Frog, hey frog, give me back my arrow!"

But the frog replied:

"Take me as your wife!"

"What are you talking about? How can I take a frog as my wife?"

"Take me — for that is your destiny."

Ivan-Tsarevich was greatly upset, but there was nothing for it. He picked up the frog and took her home. The Tsar arranged a triple wedding: his eldest son married the boyar's daughter; his second son married the merchant's daughter; and the unfortunate Ivan married the frog.

Soon the Tsar called his sons to him:

"I want to see which of your wives is the best needlewoman. Let each of them sew me a shirt by tomorrow."

The sons bowed and went to their wives.

Ivan-Tsarevich came home, sat down and hung his head. The frog jumped up and asked him:

"Why are you hanging your head, Ivan-Tsarevich? Has something bad happened?"

"My father has ordered that you sew him a shirt by tomorrow."

The frog replied:

"Don't worry, Ivan-Tsarevich. You go off to bed. In the morning everything will be as it should be."

Ivan-Tsarevich went to bed, while the frog hopped out onto the porch, shed her frog's skin and turned into Vasilísa the Wise, a maiden more beautiful than can be described even in a fairy-tale.

Vasilisa the Wise clapped her hands and shouted out:

"Nurses and nannies, hearken and come for there's work to be done! Make me by morning a shirt like my own father has."

When Ivan-Tsarevich woke in the morning, the frog was already hopping around the floor. The shirt lay on the table wrapped in a towel. Ivan-Tsarevich was delighted and took the shirt to his father. His elder brothers were just showing their wives' efforts to the Tsar. The eldest son unwrapped his shirt:

"That's a shirt fit for a lowly peasant hut."

The second son unwrapped his shirt. The Tsar said:

"That's only good for wearing to the bathhouse."

Ivan-Tsarevich unwrapped his shirt. It was embroidered with gold and silver in elaborate patterns. As soon as the Tsar saw it, he exclaimed:

"Now that is a shirt fit for a feast-day."

Ivan's two brothers went back to their homes and said to each other:

"You know, we were wrong to laugh at Ivan's wife. She is obviously not a frog, but some cunning creature…"

Soon the Tsar called his sons to him again:

"Have each of your wives bake me a loaf by tomorrow. I want to see which of them is the best cook."

Ivan-Tsarevich returned home with a heavy head. The frog asked him:

"Why so sad?"

He answered:

"You must bake the Tsar a loaf of bread by tomorrow."

"Don't worry, Ivan-Tsarevich. You go off to bed. In the morning everything will be as it should be."

The other two wives, who had laughed at the frog at first, sent an old serving-woman to watch how Ivan's bride would bake bread.

The frog could not be caught napping, though. She made dough, then broke a hole right in the top of the stove and tipped all the dough straight in. The serving-woman ran to the other brides and told them what she had seen. They began to do exactly the same.

Meanwhile the frog hopped out onto the porch, turned into Vasilisa the Wise and clapped her hands:

"Nurses and nannies, hearken and come for there's work to be done! Bake me by morning a loaf of soft white bread like I used to eat in my father's house."

When Ivan-Tsarevich woke in the morning, the loaf lay on the table. It was highly decorated with patterns pressed into the sides and a model city with gates on the top. Ivan-Tsarevich was delighted, wrapped the loaf in a cloth and took it to his father. His elder brothers were just showing their wives' efforts to the Tsar. They had tipped the dough straight into the stove as the old serving-woman had told them, and of course it came out a burnt mess. The Tsar took the loaf from his eldest son, looked at it and sent it to the servants' hall. He took the loaf from his second son and did the same. When Ivan-Tsarevich showed him his loaf, though, the Tsar exclaimed:

"This is a loaf that should be eaten only on a feast-day."

Straightaway the Tsar ordered his three sons to appear the next evening with their wives at a banquet.

Again Ivan-Tsarevich went home with a heavy heart, his head hanging low. The frog jumped up and asked him:

"Croak, croak. Why so sad, Ivan-Tsarevich? Has your father said something to upset you?"

"Frog, o frog, I cannot but be sad for my father has ordered me to bring you to the banquet tomorrow, and how can I show you to people?"

The frog replied:

"Don't worry, Ivan-Tsarevich. You go to the banquet alone, and I shall follow on. When you hear a noise like a clap of thunder, don't be afraid. If they ask, tell them: 'That's my little frog arriving in her little carriage.'"

So Ivan-Tsarevich went off to the banquet alone. His elder brothers came with their wives who were dressed in fine clothes and jewels with their cheeks rouged and their eyebrows darkened. They stood and laughed at Ivan-Tsarevich:

"Why have you not come with your wife? You could at least have brought her in a handkerchief. Where did you find such a beauty? You must have scoured the whole marsh!"

The Tsar, his sons, the two brides, and the invited guests sat down to dine at oak tables with finely-patterned table-cloths. Suddenly there was a noise like a clap of thunder. The guests took fright and sprang up from their chairs, but Ivan-Tsarevich called out:

"Do not be afraid, dear guests: It's my little frog arriving in her little carriage."

The Frog Princess

She tripped and turned, turned and tripped in such a way
that everyone was astonished. Then she swung her left hand and there
was a lake; she swung her right and there were white swans swimming
on the lake.

A golden carriage drawn by six white horses sped up to the Tsar's porch and out got Vasilisa the Wise. She was wearing a sky-blue dress spangled with stars and had a glittering tiara in her hair. She was more beautiful than can be imagined or described. She took Ivan-Tsarevich by the hand and allowed herself to be led to the oak tables with their finely-patterned table-cloths.

The guests began to eat, drink and enjoy themselves. Vasilisa the Wise drank from a glass and poured the last drops into her left sleeve. She ate some roast swan and tucked the bones into her right sleeve.

The other royal brides saw what she was doing and decided to do the same.

After the feasting was over, it came time to dance. Vasilisa the Wise took Ivan-Tsarevich and led him onto the floor. She tripped and turned, turned and tripped in such a way that everyone was astonished. Then she swung her left hand and there was a lake; she swung her right and there were white swans swimming on the lake. The Tsar and his guests were amazed.

The other brides then got up to dance. They swung their left hands and only splashed the guests; they swung their right hands and scattered bones everywhere. One of the bones struck the Tsar in the eye and he was so furious he sent them both from the hall.

Meanwhile Ivan-Tsarevich had crept out of the hall. He ran home and there he found the frog's skin. He threw it into the stove and watched as it burnt up.

When Vasilisa the Wise came home she was horrified not to find her frog's skin. She sat down on a bench, shaking her head in despair, and said to Ivan-Tsarevich:

"Oh, Ivan-Tsarevich, what have you done! If you had only waited three more days, I would have been yours for ever. Now I must bid you farewell. You must seek me at the other end of the world, where I shall be in the power of Kashchéi the Immortal."

With that Vasilisa the Wise turned into a grey cuckoo and flew out of the window. Ivan-Tsarevich wept and wept, then he took his leave and set off he knew not where to seek his wife. He walked and walked until his boots were worn through, his caftan was threadbare and the rain had ruined his hat. Then an old, old man crossed his path:

"Greetings, young sir! What are you seeking? Where are you headed?"

Ivan-Tsarevich told him about his misfortune and the old, old man told him:

"Oh, Ivan-Tsarevich, why did you burn the frog's skin? You did not put it on her and it was not for you to take it off. Vasilisa the Wise was born cleverer than her father. He grew angry with her for that reason and ordered her to spend three years as a frog. Well, there's nothing more to be done. Here, take this ball of yarn. Follow it boldly wherever it rolls."

Ivan-Tsarevich thanked the old, old man and set off after the ball of yarn. The ball kept rolling and he followed it. Once in the open countryside he came across a bear. Ivan-Tsarevich took aim and was about to kill the bear when it spoke to him in a human voice:

"Don't kill me, Ivan-Tsarevich. I shall be of use to you."

Ivan-Tsarevich dropped his bow and spared the bear. He walked on and, glancing up, saw a drake flying past. He took aim, but the drake spoke to him in a human voice:

"Don't kill me, Ivan-Tsarevich. I shall be of use to you."

Ivan-Tsarevich spared the drake and walked on. A hare ran across his path. Again Ivan-Tsarevich snatched up his bow and was about to shoot when the hare spoke to him in a human voice:

"Don't kill me, Ivan-Tsarevich. I shall be of use to you."

He spared the hare and walked on. He came to the deep blue sea and there on the sand he saw a pike. It was barely breathing and gasped out:

"Ivan-Tsarevich, spare me! Throw me back into the deep blue sea!"

He tossed the pike back into the sea and walked on along the shore. After a time the ball of yarn brought him to a forest. There he found a hut on chicken's legs, turning around.

Ivan-Tsarevich called out:

"Hut, o hut, stand as your mother placed you of old: your back to the trees, your front to me!"

The hut turned so its back was to the trees and its front to Ivan-Tsarevich. He climbed inside and there on the stove, on the ninth brick, he saw Bába-Yagá with her leg of bone. Her teeth were on the shelf and her nose had grown into the ceiling.

"Why have you come calling, my fine young man?" Baba-Yaga asked him. "Are you looking for an adventure, or looking to avoid one?"

But Ivan-Tsarevich replied:

"You old hag, you should give me food and drink and let me use the bathhouse, before you start your questioning."

Baba-Yaga let him use the bathhouse, gave him food and drink and made him up a bed. Then Ivan-Tsarevich told her that he was looking for his wife, Vasilisa the Wise.

"I know, I know," Baba-Yaga said. "Your wife is now in the power of Kashchei the Immortal. It will be no easy matter to recover her, as Kashchei is hard to deal with. His death is at the tip of a needle; that needle is in an egg; that egg is in a duck; that duck is in a hare; that hare sits in a stone box; that stone box rests in a tall oak; and Kashchei guards that oak with all his might."

Ivan-Tsarevich spent the night in Baba-Yaga's hut and in the morning she showed him where the tall oak grew. He set off walking and eventually he came to the oak. He looked up and there indeed in its branches was a stone box, way out of reach.

Suddenly, from out of nowhere, a bear ran up and tore the oak out by the roots. The stone box fell down and broke open. Out sprang a hare and ran off as fast as its legs could carry it. But another hare went chasing after it, caught it and tore it to pieces. Out flew a duck and climbed way up into the sky. But a drake dived onto the duck and struck it so hard that it dropped the egg. The egg fell into the deep blue sea…

At that moment Ivan-Tsarevich burst into tears — how would he find the egg in the sea? Suddenly a pike swam in to the shore with the egg in its mouth. Ivan-Tsarevich took the egg, broke it, pulled out the needle and began with all his strength to snap off the tip. He strained and strained, and Kashchei the Immortal writhed and dashed about. For all Kashchei's struggling, Ivan-Tsarevich managed to break the tip of the needle and Kashchei had to die.

Ivan-Tsarevich went into Kashchei's palace of white stone and Vasilisa the Wise came running out to meet him. She kissed him on his sweet lips. Ivan-Tsarevich and Vasilisa the Wise returned home where both lived happily to a ripe old age.

The Seven Simeons, Seven Labourers

Once upon a time there were seven brothers, the seven Simeons, seven labourers.

One day they went out to plough and sow grain. The Tsar happened to be riding by with his general. He looked at the field and was astonished at the sight of the seven labourers.

"What's that?" he asked. "Seven ploughmen in a single field, all the same height and all with the same features. Find out who those labourers are."

The Tsar's servants hurried into the field and brought the seven Simeons before the Tsar.

"Well," said the Tsar, "tell me: who are you and what are you doing?"

The young men replied:

"We are seven brothers, the seven Simeons, seven labourers. We till the land of our father and grandfather and each of us is trained in his own craft."

"Well," said the Tsar, "and what crafts might those be?"

The eldest brother said: "I can build a pillar of iron from the earth to the sky."

The second said: "I can climb that pillar and look in all directions to see what is happening."

The third said: "I am Simeon the Seafarer. I can build a ship in a trice; I'll take it across the sea, sailing fast and free."

"I am Simeon the Marksman," said the fourth. "I can hit a fly in flight with my arrow."

"I am Simeon the Star-Counter. I count the stars down to the very last one."

"And I am Simeon the Grain-Grower. In a single day I plough and sow and reap the harvest."

"And who might you be?" the Tsar asked the youngest.

"I, Your Majesty, sing and dance and play the pipe."

Then the Tsar's general said:

"Your Majesty, we have great need of labourers, but send the dancing piper away. We do not need his kind. They only eat our bread and drink our *kvass** to no benefit."

"Very likely," said the Tsar.

But the youngest Simeon bowed to the Tsar and said:

"Allow me, Your Majesty, to demonstrate my craft by playing a tune on the horn."

"Why not," the Tsar replied. "Play one last time and then get out of my kingdom."

At that the youngest Simeon took up a horn made of birch-bark and launched into a lively Russian dance. And in an instant everyone was dancing, their legs flying to and fro. The Tsar was dancing, his boyars were dancing and the guards were dancing too. The horses started dancing in their stalls; the cows tapped their hooves in the barns. The chickens and cockerels jigged about. But the Tsar's general capered more than anyone. The sweat poured out of him, his beard shook and tears were already running down his cheeks.

Then the Tsar shouted out:

"Stop playing! I haven't the strength to dance any more!"

The youngest Simeon said:

"Take a rest, good people. But you, general, with your wicked tongue and unkind eye can go on dancing."

So everyone stopped, apart from the general. He danced on and on, until he dropped. He lay on the ground gasping like a fish out of water. Then the youngest Simeon put aside his birch-bark horn.

"That," he announced, "is my craft."

The Tsar laughed, but the general kept a furious silence.

Then the Tsar said:

"Well, eldest Simeon, now show us your skill."

The eldest Simeon took a fifteen-*pood*** hammer and knocked together an iron pillar from the earth to the deep blue sky. The second Simeon climbed up the pillar and looked in all directions.

The Tsar shouted up to him:

---

* Kvass – a kind of drink made from fermenting rye or barely, very mildly alcoholic.

** Pood – an old Russian weight, 16,38 kilogrammes or just over 36 pounds.

"Tell us what you can see!"

The second Simeon answered:

"I can see the ships sailing the sea. I can see the grain ripening in the fields."

"What else?"

"I can see across the great sea, on the island of Buyan, Yeléna the Beautiful sitting by the window of the golden palace and weaving a silken carpet."

"What is she like?" the Tzar asked.

"More beautiful than can be imagined or described. A tiara on her head and a tiny pearl on each of her hairs."

As soon as he heard that, the Tsar was determined to have Yelena the Beautiful as his bride. He wanted to send ambassadors to court her. The wicked general put in his own suggestion:

"Send the seven Simeons to bring back Yelena the Beautiful, Your Majesty. They are men of great skill. And if they fail to bring her back, have them executed."

"Why not, I'll do it!" said the Tsar.

And so he ordered the seven Simeons to go to the fabulous island and bring back Yelena the Beautiful.

"And if you fail," he threatened, "you will answer for it with your necks."

So the brothers had no choice. Simeon the Seafarer took a sharp axe and in a trice he had built a ship, fitted, rigged and launched it. They loaded the ship with all manner of goods — different precious gifts, and the Tsar ordered the wicked general to sail with the brothers to keep an eye on them. At that the general turned very pale, but he had no choice but to go. He that mischief hatches mischief catches.

They all got on board the ship. The sails flapped, the waves lapped, and they crossed the great sea to the island of Buyan.

They came to Yelena the Beautiful, gave her the rich presents and began wooing her on the Tsar's behalf. Yelena the Beautiful took the presents and examined them.

While she was doing so, the wicked general whispered in her ear:

"Don't go, Princess, the Tsar is old and weak. Wolves howl and bears roam in his kingdom."

Yelena the Beautiful grew angry and ordered the brothers out of her sight. Now what could they do?

"Well, brothers," said the youngest Simeon, "go to the ship, stock up with grain, raise the sails, make ready to leave, and my part shall be to bring the princess."

Within the hour Simeon the Grain-Grower had ploughed the sandy shore, sowed rye, reaped his harvest and baked bread enough for the whole journey.

Meanwhile the youngest Simeon went back to the palace. Yelena the Beautiful was sitting by the window and weaving a silken carpet. The youngest Simeon sat down on a bench beneath the window and began talking in this vein:

"It is very fine and pleasant here, beyond the sea, on the island of Buyan, but in Mother Russia it is a hundred times better. Our meadows are green and our rivers blue. We have fields that go on for ever, white birches by the backwaters, sky-blue flowers in the meadows. With us dusk melts into dawn; the moon grazes the stars in the sky. We have dews of honey and rivers of silver. The shepherd comes out into the green meadow, starts playing his birch-bark horn, and, whether you like it or not, you just have to follow him."

With that, the youngest Simeon began playing his birch-bark horn. Yelena the Beautiful came to the doorway of the golden palace. Simeon walked off through the garden, still playing, and Yelena the Beautiful followed him. He left the garden and she left the garden. He walked across the fields and she walked across the fields. He came down to the shore and she came down to the shore. He boarded the ship and she boarded the ship.

As soon as she was aboard, the brothers quickly cast off, turned the ship and headed out to sea.

Simeon stopped playing his horn and immediately Yelena the Beautiful came out of her trance.

She looked around and realised she was out at sea, far from the island of Buyan. Yelena the Beautiful struck the wooden deck of the ship and flew up into the heavens as a pale blue star that was soon lost among all the others. Simeon the Star-Counter dashed out and counted all the stars shining in the sky so as to find the new one. Simeon the Marksman dashed out and shot a gold arrow at that star. The star tumbled onto the wooden deck and turned back into Yelena the Beautiful.

Then the youngest Simeon said to her:

"Don't run away from us, princess. There's is nowhere you can hide from us. If it is such a torment for you to sail with us, we had better take you back home, for all the Tsar will have our heads because of it."

Yelena the Beautiful took pity on the youngest Simeon:

"I won't let you lose your head on my account, Simeon the Singer. I'd rather sail to the old Tsar."

So they sailed on day after day. The youngest Simeon did not stir from the princess's side, and Yelena the Beautiful never took her eyes off him.

The wicked general noticed all this and forged his wicked plans. By now they were already close to home, the coast came into view. The general called the brothers together on deck and gave them a goblet of sweet wine:

"Let us drink, fellow voyagers, to our native land!"

The brothers drank the sweet wine, lay down on the deck wherever they found space and fell fast asleep. Neither thunder, nor storm, nor their own mother's tears could have woken them because the general had mixed a powerful sleeping draught into the wine.

Only Yelena the Beautiful and the youngest Simeon had not drunk the wine.

And so they arrived back in their native land. The elder brothers continued to sleep like logs. The youngest Simeon made Yelena the Beautiful ready to meet the Tsar. Both were sighing and crying, unwilling to part, but there was nothing to be done. If you have not given you word, stand to your sword, but if you have given your word, stand by that.

Meanwhile the wicked general had run on ahead to the Tsar and fallen at his feet, saying: "Your Majesty, the youngest Simeon has evil intentions towards you. He wants to kill you and take the princess for himself. Have him executed."

As soon as Simeon and the princess presented themselves to the Tsar, he took her into his palace with every honour and ordered his men to throw him into prison.

The youngest Simeon shouted out:

"My brothers, the six Simeons! Help your youngest brother!"

The brothers continued sleeping like logs.

The youngest Simeon was thrown into prison and fettered with heavy chains.

In the morning they brought the youngest Simeon out to meet his cruel death. The princess wept, shedding pearly tears. The wicked general smirked.

Then the youngest Simeon spoke out:

"O cruel Tsar, keep the hallowed custom and grant a condemned man's last request: let me play on my horn one last time."

The wicked general shouted:

"No, Your Majesty, don't let him!"

But the Tsar said:

"I will not break the custom of my forefathers. Play, Simeon, but be quick, my executioners are tired of waiting and their sharp swords have grown blunt."

The youngest brother played his birch-bark horn.

The sound carried across hills and vales until it reached the ship. His elder brothers heard it, woke up, stretched and said:

"That must mean that our youngest brother is in trouble!"

They ran to the Tsar's court. The executioners had just picked up their sharp swords to lop off Simeon's head when, out of nowhere, his elder brothers appeared: Simeon the Builder, Simeon the Sharp-Eyed, Simeon the Grain-Grower, Simeon the Seafarer, Simeon the Star-Counter and Simeon the Marksman.

This terrifying group advanced on the old Tsar:

"Let our youngest brother go free and give him Yelena the Beautiful."

The Tsar cowered and said:

"Have your youngest brother, and the princess into the bargain. I didn't like her anyway. Be quick and take her away."

And then there was a feast to which everyone was invited. They ate and drank and sang songs. Then the youngest Simeon took up his horn and launched into a dance tune.

The Tsar danced and the princess danced; the boyars danced and the boyars' daughters danced. The horses started dancing in their stalls; the cows tapped their hooves in the barns. The chickens and cockerels jigged about.

But the general capered more than anyone. He danced on and on, until he dropped down dead.

So the youngest brother and the princess were married and everyone has gone back to work. Simeon the Builder puts up houses; Simeon the Grain-Grower sows; Simeon the Seafarer plies the seas; Simeon the Star-Counter keeps track of the stars; Simeon the Sharp-Eyed and Simeon the Marksman protect the land. There is work enough for all in Mother Russia.

And the youngest Simeon sings songs and plays his horn. He keeps everyone happy and helps them to do their work.

Tereshechka

Once upon a time there was an old man and an old woman. They had lived a lifetime together, but never had any children.

So they took a little log, swaddled it like a baby and began to rock it gently singing all the while:

"Sleep, Teréshechka; close your eyes.
The swallows all have gone to bed.
The martins too lay down their heads.
The fox and the vixen both are asleep
So are the cows, so are the sheep.
Sleep, Tereshechka; close your eyes,
As we sing this lullaby."

They rocked and rocked, sang and sang, and instead of a log they had a little son — Tereshechka, a real delight.

The boy grew up and when he was of an age to look after himself, the old man made him a boat. He painted the boat white and the paddles red.

Tereshechka got into his new boat and said:

"Boat, o boat, carry me far away!
Boat, o boat, carry me far away!"

And the boat did indeed carry him far away. Tereshechka began to catch fish and his mother brought him milk and cheese.

She would come down to the shore and call out:

"Tereshechka, Tereshechka, come over here!
I've brought you food and drink, my dear!"

Tereshechka could hear his mother calling far out on the water and came in to the shore. His mother took the fish he had caught, gave him food, drink and a change of clothes and left him to go back to his fishing.

A witch found out about all this. She came down to the shore and called out in her terrible voice:

"Tereshechka, Tereshechka, come over here!
I've brought you food and drink, my dear!"

Tereshechka realised it was not his mother's voice, though, and said:

"Boat, o boat, carry me far away!
For it's not mother's voice I hear today!"

Then the old witch ran to the forge and had the smith beat her throat into shape so that her voice sounded just like Tereshechka's mother.

After the smith had done his work, the witch went down to the shore again and called out in her new voice:

"Tereshechka, Tereshechka, come over here!
I've brought you food and drink, my dear!"

This time Tereshechka failed to notice the deception and came in to the shore. The witch seized him, popped him in a sack and ran off.

She carried him to her hut on chicken's legs and told her daughter Aliónka to stoke up the stove and roast Tereshechka. Meanwhile she went off to see what else she could catch.

Alionka stoked the stove until it was as hot as she could get it, then said to Tereshechka:

"Climb on the shovel."

He lay down on the shovel, but spread his arms and legs wide so that he would not fit in the oven. She shouted at him:

"Lie properly!"

"I don't know how — you show me."

"Lie down like a cat going to sleep."

"You'd better lie down yourself and show me."

Alionka got onto the shovel and quick as a flash Tereshechka popped her in the oven and shut the door. Then he climbed out of the hut and up a tall oak-tree.

The witch came back, opened the oven and pulled out her daughter Alionka. She ate her all up and gnawed on the bones. Then she went outside and began rolling on the grass.

She rolled this way and that, repeating to herself:

"Rolling around, can't keep to my feet, I've eaten my fill of Tereshechka's meat."

Then Tereshechka called down from his oak:

"Rolling around, can't keep to your feet, you've eaten your fill of Alionka's meat!"

The witch said:

"What was that? The wind in the leaves?"

Again she repeated:

"Rolling around, can't keep to my feet, I've eaten my fill of Tereshechka's meat."

And Tereshechka called down:

"Rolling around, can't keep to your feet, you've eaten your fill of Alionka's meat!"

The witch looked up and spotted him in the tall oak. She hurled herself at the tree and began gnawing at it. She gnawed and gnawed until her top front teeth broke. Then she ran to the forge:

"Smith, smith, make me a pair of iron teeth!"

The smith made her a pair of teeth.

The witch came back and started gnawing at the oak again. She gnawed and gnawed until her bottom front teeth broke. Then she ran to the forge:

"Smith, smith, make me another pair of iron teeth!"

The smith made her another pair of teeth.

The witch came back and started gnawing at the oak again. She worked so hard and fast that the splinters simply flew. The oak was already swaying and on the point of falling.

Tereshechka was wondering what on earth he could do when he saw the swan-geese flying by. He called out to them:

"Swans, swans, geese, my dears!
Carry me away from here!
Take me back to father; take me back to mother!"

But the swan-geese answered:

"Honk, honk, there are more behind, hungrier than us. They will take you."

The witch kept gnawing and gnawing. She glanced up at Tereshechka, licked her lips and went back to work.

Another skein of birds flew past. Tereshechka called out to them:

"Swans, swans, geese, my dears!
Carry me away from here!
Take me back to father; take me back to mother!"

But the swan-geese answered:
"Honk, honk, there is a pecked gosling behind. He will take you and bring you home."
By now the witch had nearly finished. Another few bites and the oak would fall.
The pecked gosling flew by. Tereshechka called out to him:
"My dear swan-goose, carry me away from here! Take me back to father, take me back to mother!"
The pecked gosling took pity on him, sat him on his neck, spread his wings and flew away.
They flew to Tereshechka's house and landed on the grass outside.
The old woman was following the old custom and cooking pancakes in Tereshechka's memory, as she believed him to be dead.
"Here's a pancake for you, old man, and here's one for me."
Tereshechka called in through the window:
"And where's my pancake?"
The old woman heard him and said:
"Just a moment, old man. Who's that asking for a pancake?"
The old man went outside, saw Tereshechka and brought him in. How they hugged and kissed each other!
They fed and watered the pecked gosling until he became a fine goose, then they let him go. From that time on he spread his wings with pride and led the flock far and wide. Tereshechka was ever on his mind, as he repaid kindness by being kind.

The King of the Sea and Vasilisa the Wise

Once upon a time, in a faraway country, there lived a tsar and his tsarina who had no children. The tsar went off on a long journey to distant lands and while he was away the tsarina gave birth to a son, whom she called Ivan-Tsarevich, or Prince Ivan. The tsar, however, did not know he had become a father.

He began his return journey and, as he approached his own country, the sun began to beat down, and the air was hot and dry. The tsar was tormented by thirst and would have given anything just for a drink. He looked around and not far away he spotted a large lake. He rode down to the lake, jumped from his horse, lay down flat on the bank and began to lap up the icy cold water. He drank and drank, never suspecting the trouble he was in — for the King of the Sea had seized him by the beard.

"Let me go," the tsar begged.

"No I will not. How dare you drink my water without permission!"

"I'll give you anything you ask, only let me go."

"Give me the thing that you do not know at home."

The tsar thought and thought — what was there at home that he did not know? He was sure that he knew everything, that everything was familiar — and so he agreed. He lifted his head and his beard came free of the water. He got up, mounted his horse and returned home.

As he rode up, the tsarina came out to meet him, holding their son. She was full of joy, but, when he heard of his son's birth, the tsar shed bitter tears. He told the tsarina what had happened to him and they wept together. But there was nothing to be done — it's no use, as they say, crying over spilt milk.

They went back to their life together. The prince seemed to grow as they watched and before any time at all had passed he was a fine young man.

"However long we keep him, we shall have to give him up in the end," the tsar thought and decided to have done with it. He took Ivan-Tsarevich by the hand and led him straight to the fateful lake.

"Search here for my ring," he told him. "I dropped it here yesterday."

He left the prince alone and went back home.

Ivan began looking for the ring. As he walked along the lakeshore, an old woman came from the opposite direction.

"Where are you going, Ivan-Tsarevich."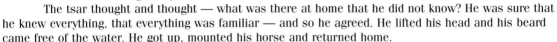

"Don't bother me, old witch. Be off with you, things are bad enough already."

"In that case, good day to you." The old woman walked away.

Then Ivan-Tsarevich thought better of what he had done. "Why was I rude to the old woman? I'll call her back. Old people can be quick-witted and cunning. She might tell me something useful." And he shouted after her:

"Come back, good woman, forgive me my hasty words! I spoke out of vexation. My father left me here to search for his ring and I cannot find it for all my looking!"

"It's not on account of a ring that you are here. Your father has given you up to the King of the Sea. The King will come out and take you back with him to his underwater kingdom."

The prince burst into tears.

"Don't despair, Ivan-Tsarevich! Your luck may still change, if you listen well to what an old woman tells you. Hide behind that currant-bush and stay quiet. A dozen doves will land here, all beautiful maidens, and they will be followed by a thirteenth. All will go to bathe in the lake. While they are bathing, you take the thirteenth's shift and be sure to keep it until she gives you her ring. If you fail, you will be lost for ever. A high wall of stakes, fully ten versts long, surrounds the King of the Sea's palace, and on the top of each stake there is a head. One alone remains unoccupied. Don't let your head end up on it!"

Ivan-Tsarevich thanked the old woman, got down behind the currant bush and waited for what would happen.

Suddenly twelve doves came out of the air and, as they touched the earth, they turned into

beautiful maidens, each fairer in face and body than can be imagined or described. They shook off their dresses and entered the lake, where they splashed and played, laughed and sang.

Soon a thirteenth dove flew down and turned into a beautiful maiden as it touched the ground. She threw the shift off her milk-white body and went to bathe. This maiden was fairer and lovelier than all the rest!

For a long time Ivan-Tsarevich was unable to tear his eyes away from her. He stared and stared, but then he remembered what the old woman had told him. He crept up and took her shift.

The beautiful maiden came out of the water and could not find her shift. Someone must have taken it. All the maidens looked, but it was nowhere to be found.

"Search no more, dear sisters! Fly away home. It is my fault. I did not keep my eye on it and I must take the blame."

The beautiful maiden sisters struck the ground, turned back into doves, spread their wings and flew away. Left alone, the maiden looked all around and said aloud:

"Come out with my shift, whoever you are. If you are an old man you will be like a father to me. If you are of middle age, you will be a favourite brother. And if you are of my own age you will be my dear sweetheart."

As soon as the words were out, Ivan-Tsarevich showed himself. She gave him her gold ring and said:

"Oh, Ivan-Tsarevich, why have you been so long in coming? The King of the Sea is furious with you. There is the road that leads to the underwater kingdom: follow it and don't be afraid. You will find me there too, for I am Vasilísa the Wise, daughter of the King of the Sea."

Vasilisa turned herself into a bird and flew off, leaving the prince alone.

Ivan-Tsarevich made his way into the underwater kingdom. He saw that the light is the same there as with us. There are fields and meadows and green groves and the sun shines warm.

He presented himself to the King of the Sea and the King shouted at him:

"Why have you been so long in coming? To make up for it, here is what you have to do: I have piece of waste land thirty versts long and thirty wide, full of pits, gullies and sharp stones. Tomorrow I want to see it as flat as my hand and sown with rye that by early morning has grown so high that a jackdaw can hide in it. And if you fail, your head will fly from your shoulders!"

Ivan-Tsarevich left the King of the Sea and burst into tears. Vasilisa the Wise saw him from her room high in the palace and called to him:

"Greetings, Ivan-Tsarevich! Why so miserable?"

"How can I be anything else but miserable?" the prince replied. "The King of the Sea has ordered me to fill in the pits and gullies, remove the stones, and sow the field with rye that by morning should be so high that a jackdaw can hide in it."

"That is no trouble, the trouble is yet to come. Lie down and sleep peacefully. In the morning everything will be as it should be."

Ivan-Tsarevich went to bed, and Vasilisa the Wise came out onto the porch and shouted in a loud voice:

"Hey, my loyal servants! Level the deep pits, remove the sharp stones and sow the field with rye so that it ripens by morning."

Ivan-Tsarevich awoke with the dawn. He looked out and everything was done: no pits or gullies, the field was as smooth as your hand and full of rye tall enough to hide a jackdaw.

He went and reported to the King of the Sea.

"I thank you for that service," the King said. "Here is another task: I have three hundred shocks, each containing three hundred sheaves — all of fine corn. Take out all the corn, down to the very last grain, for me by tomorrow, but do not break up the shocks or take the sheaves apart. If you fail, your head will fly from your shoulders!"

"Yes, Your Majesty," Ivan-Tsarevich replied. Again he turned and went away in tears.

The King of the Sea
and Vasilisa the Wise

*B*ut Vasilisa the Wise and Ivan-Tsarevich were already far away. They drove their swift-footed steeds on without pausing to rest.

"Why so miserable?" Vasilisa the Wise asked him.

"How can I be anything else but miserable? The King of the Sea has ordered me to collect all the corn in a single night, without losing a single grain, breaking up the shocks or taking the sheaves apart."

"That is no trouble, the trouble is yet to come. Lie down and sleep peacefully. In the morning everything will be as it should be."

Ivan-Tsarevich went to bed, and Vasilisa the Wise came out onto the porch and shouted in a loud voice:

"Hey, you creeping ants! However many of you there are in the world, all come here and bring the corn from my father's shocks, down to the very last grain."

In the morning the King of the Sea summoned Ivan-Tsarevich.

"Well, have you performed that task?"

"I have, Your Majesty."

"Let's go and see."

They went to the threshing barn. All the shocks were still standing whole and unbroken. They went to the granaries. All the bins were full to the brim with grain.

"Thank you, son," said the King of the Sea. "If you can make me a church of pure wax by tomorrow morning, that will be your last task."

Again Ivan-Tsarevich went away with tears in his eyes.

"Why so miserable?" Vasilisa the Wise asked him from her high window.

"How can I be anything else but miserable? The King of the Sea has ordered me to build a church of pure wax in a single night."

"That is no trouble, the trouble is yet to come. Lie down and sleep peacefully. In the morning everything will be as it should be."

Ivan-Tsarevich went to bed, and Vasilisa the Wise came out onto the porch and shouted in a loud voice:

"Hey, you busy bees! However many of you there are in the world, all come here and build a church out of pure wax by the morning."

In the morning Ivan-Tsarevich awoke, looked out and there was a church of pure wax. He went and reported to the King of the Sea.

"Thank you, Ivan-Tsarevich. Of all the servants I have ever had, none has pleased me as greatly as you. For that you shall be my heir, the guardian of the whole realm, and choose any of my thirteen daughters to be your wife."

Ivan-Tsarevich chose Vasilisa the Wise. They were married at once and the feasting and celebrations went on for three whole days.

After some time had passed, Ivan-Tsarevich began to miss his parents and to long to see the holy land of Russia once more.

"Why so miserable, Ivan-Tsarevich?"

"Oh, Vasilisa, I am missing my father and my mother; I want to go back to holy Russia."

"There we are, the trouble has come! If we leave, there will be a great hunt for us. The King of the Sea will be furious and have us put to death. We shall have to be cunning."

Vasilisa spat in three corners of their room, locked the door and hurried off with Ivan-Tsarevich in the direction of holy Russia.

Early the next day messengers came to summon the young couple to the King of the Sea. They knocked on the door and called out:

"Wake up. Get up. The King has summoned you!"

"It's still early. We haven't finished sleeping. Come back later," one drop of spit answered.

The messengers went away, waited for an hour or two and then knocked again:

"It's time to stop sleeping and get up!"

"Wait a little. We're getting up and dressing," the second drop of spit replied.

The messengers came back a third time to say that the King was angry because they were taking so much time.

"We're just coming," the third drop of spit answered.

The messengers waited and waited. They knocked again and when they got no response, they broke down the door and found the room empty.

When they told the King that the young couple had fled, he flew into a rage and raised a great hunt for them.

But Vasilisa the Wise and Ivan-Tsarevich were already far away. They drove their swift-footed steeds on without pausing to rest.

"Ivan-Tsarevich, put your ear to the ground and listen whether the King of the Sea has sent his people after us."

Ivan-Tsarevich leapt from his horse, put his ear to the ground and said:

"I can hear talking and the beat of hooves."

"They are coming after us," said Vasilisa the Wise and instantly changed the horses into a green meadow, Ivan-Tsarevich into an old shepherd and herself into a gently grazing sheep.

The pursuers rode up to them:

"Hey, old shepherd, have you seen a fine young man and a beautiful girl ride by here?"

"No, I haven't, good sirs," Ivan-Tsarevich replied. "In the forty years I have been tending my sheep here, not a single bird has flown by, not a single beast has run by."

The pursuers turned back:

"Your Majesty, we found no-one on the road and saw only an old shepherd tending a sheep."

"Why didn't you seize them — that was Ivan and Vasilisa," the King shouted and sent his men out again.

Meanwhile Ivan-Tsarevich and Vasilisa the Wise were back on their horses and riding like the wind.

"Ivan-Tsarevich, put your ear to the ground and listen whether the King of the Sea has sent his people after us."

Ivan-Tsarevich leapt from his horse, put his ear to the ground and said:

"I can hear talking and the beat of hooves."

"They are coming after us," said Vasilisa the Wise. She changed herself into a church, Ivan-Tsarevich into an old priest and the horses into trees.

The pursuers rode up to them:

"Hey, father, have you seen a shepherd and a sheep go by here?"

""No, I haven't, good sirs. In the forty years I have been working in this church, not a single bird has flown by, not a single beast has run by."

The pursuers turned back:

"Your Majesty, we could not find the shepherd and the sheep anywhere. All that we saw on the way was a church with an old priest."

"Why didn't you smash down the church and seize the priest? It was Ivan and Vasilisa!" the King of the Sea fumed and mounted up himself to chase after Ivan-Tsarevich and Vasilisa the Wise.

Meanwhile they were even further on.

Again Vasilisa the Wise said:

"Ivan-Tsarevich, put your ear to the ground and listen whether the King of the Sea has sent his people after us."

Ivan-Tsarevich leapt from his horse, put his ear to the ground and said:

"I can hear talking and the beat of hooves stronger than before."

"It's the King himself riding after us."

Vasilisa the Wise turned the horses into a lake, herself into a duck and Ivan-Tsarevich into a drake.

The King of the Sea rode up to the lake and immediately realised who the duck and drake really were. He struck the ground and turned himself into an eagle. The eagle tried to kill them, but could not manage it… Each time he plunged down on them, at the last instant they dived beneath the water. Again and again he attacked, again and again they slipped away. In the end the King rode back to his underwater kingdom. Vasilisa the Wise and Ivan-Tsarevich waited a good while and then rode on to holy Russia.

Eventually they came to Ivan-Tsarevich's own land.

"Wait for me here in this little wood," he told Vasilisa the Wise. "I will go ahead and announce our arrival to father and mother."

"You will forget me, Ivan-Tsarevich!"

"No, I won't."

"You will, Ivan-Tsarevich. Remember me at least when two doves begin tapping on the window."

Ivan-Tsarevich entered the palace. His parents saw him and rushed to embrace him. In his happiness the prince forgot about Vasilisa the Wise.

He lived one day with his father and mother, then a second, and on the third he began thinking of courting some princess.

Vasilisa the Wise went into the town and took work with a woman who baked the communion bread. They began to prepare the Host and she took two small pieces of dough, fashioned them into doves and put them in the oven.

"Guess what will become of those doves, mistress."

"What will become of them? We'll eat them, of course."

"No, you guessed wrong!"

Vasilisa the Wise opened the oven, flung the window wide, and in an instant the doves spread their wings, flew straight to the palace and began to tap on the windows. Try as they might, the tsar's servants could not drive them off.

Then Ivan-Tsarevich remembered about Vasilisa the Wise. He sent messengers out in all directions to find her and discovered her with the woman who baked the Host. He took her by the hands, kissed her on the lips and brought her to his mother and father. The young couple moved into the palace and they all lived happily ever after.

ЧАЕПИЕ В ПОДМОСКОВЬЕ

CONTENS

Introduction by Abram Raskin
English translation by Paul Williams
Illustrations by Alexey Orleansky (www.palekh.itgo.com)
Designed by Piotr Kanaykin
Managing editor: Maria Lyzhenkova
Computer type-setting by Yelena Morozova
Colour proofs by Liubov Kornilova and Vladimir Glazkov
Editor-in-Chief: Sergei Vesnin

ISBN 5-8194-0019-4

Printed and bound by the Ivan Fiodorov Printing Company, St Petersburg (No 2778)